Glamour! * Talent!

* Stardom! *

* Fame and fortune *
could be one step away!

Welcome to
Fame
School

For another fix of

Fame School

read

Fame School

Summer Spectacular

Cindy Jefferies

USBORNE

For the whole wonderful team at Usborne.
This one's for you!

First published in 2009 by Usborne Publishing Ltd., Usborne House,
83-85 Saffron Hill, London EC1N 8RT, England. www.usborne.com

A CIP catalogue record for this book is available from the British Library.

1 Holiday Time

"Wait, Chloe! Wait a moment!"

Chloe Tompkins paused. She was just about to cram a couple of bags into the boot of her parents' car, but as soon as she heard her name she put them down, and turned round to see who was calling her. It was Lolly Lowther, one of the famous model twins, who shared a room with Chloe and Tara Fitzgerald at Rockley Park School. Like Chloe, the twins were learning to be singers, whilst Tara was studying bass guitar.

Lolly squeezed her way through the throng of students and parents to reach Chloe outside the boarding house. It was always a crush on the last afternoon of term, when parents arrived for the end of term concert, before taking their children home for the holidays.

The end of the summer term was the most frantic of all, because the students had to take every single thing they owned back home. Rockley Park was a school for budding singers, dancers and musicians, and it held lots of residential music courses during the summer holidays. Mrs. Pinto, the housemistress, had threatened to throw away anything left behind, because the bedrooms would be needed. The students knew that she meant what she said.

"Here! I forgot to give you these." Lolly was holding a pile of clothes in her hand.

"Oh Lolly, are you sure? Does your mum mind you giving them away?" said Chloe.

Lolly laughed. "I don't think we've got room for even one more top in the car," she said. "And Mum is going spare, because Pop just asked if she could go shopping for a new swimsuit on the way home!"

Chloe smiled. "Surely Pop can wait a couple of days?"

"She's going to have to!" said Lol if you'd like these tops, Chloe, have them. designers must have sent two of each colour, and Pop and I can't wear them *all*."

Chloe eyed the tops excitedly. There were some gorgeous colours in the pile. Designers often sent the twins clothes from their latest collections. They'd passed some on to Chloe before. She could never have afforded to buy such expensive clothes herself so it was fantastic to have them.

"Well if you're sure…"

Lolly thrust them into her arms. "You'll be doing me a big favour," she laughed. "Besides, they'll look brilliant on you!"

Chloe felt a shiver of anticipation. "Thanks!" she said, beaming at Lolly. "I can't wait to try them on!"

Chloe and Lolly looked at each other. They were best friends at Rockley Park, and it would be quite sad for them not to see each other for the whole summer.

"I had the *best* time at the concert," sighed Chloe.

"We all performed well, didn't we?" said Lolly. "There

were no mix-ups, and all our teachers seemed pleased. I enjoyed it too."

"I can't believe how long it's going to be until we're back here again," said Chloe. "It seems an *age*."

"Well, have a great summer with your family," Lolly said, giving Chloe a last hug. "I'll miss you, *and* Rockley Park as well."

"Me too," said Chloe, hugging Lolly back.

"At least you'll be able to hang out with Danny," Lolly said. "Pity me, stuck with my sister all summer long."

Chloe laughed. She knew Lolly didn't mean it. She got on very well with Pop as a rule. But Lolly was right about Danny. He lived in Chloe's town. If Chloe missed Rockley Park too much she could easily arrange to meet the drummer for a chat.

"Well, bye then," said Chloe reluctantly. "See you in September."

Before Lolly could reply, her twin sister appeared.

"Come *on*," said Pop. "Mum says she's going without you unless you come this *minute*. Bye, Chloe,"

she added, giving her a quick hug. "Have a great time."
Pop dragged her sister through the crush and, with a
last wave, they were gone.

Chloe put the bags in the car boot, and got into the
back seat with an armful of tops.

"All set?" asked her dad.

"All set," agreed Chloe, leaning back into her seat.

Her little brother, Ben, was strapped in next to her.

"Let me see," he said, pulling at the clothes.

"Oh, Ben!" complained Chloe. Then she stopped.
He wouldn't spoil them, and she didn't want to be
mean. It had been ages since they'd seen each other,
and she'd missed him, as she did every term.

"They're just some tops that Lolly gave me," she
explained. "Which colour do you like best?"

"This one," he said, "I want this one."

"Well I think it'll be a bit big for you," said Chloe, but
Ben was already dragging a red T-shirt out of the pile.
He struggled to get it over his head.

"Too big!" he announced.

Chloe giggled. "Told you!" she said and helped him

out of it. "Never mind. The one you're wearing is very nice, and it's got some red on it too."

There were so many cars that it took quite a few minutes to get onto the main drive. While they waited, Chloe spotted Tara getting into a taxi and gave her a wave. Tara's parents hardly ever had time to collect her themselves, which Chloe thought was rather sad.

At last, Chloe's car turned out of the gates and onto the main road.

"Soon be home for the holidays!" said Chloe's mum with a happy smile. "It'll be such fun to have you back with us. We've missed you, Chloe."

"Missed you!" said little Ben earnestly.

Chloe smiled and ruffled his hair. "Me too," she told him. "But don't worry, Ben. This time I'm going to be home for weeks and weeks!"

It was quite a long drive to Chloe's home. Ben soon fell asleep, and Chloe sat quietly, clutching her tops. She was looking forward to sleeping in her own bedroom again, and to seeing Jess, her best friend from home. They had been at different schools for a couple of years now, but they always caught up with each other in the holidays. They'd known each other since they were babies, and Chloe couldn't wait to see her again. In fact, she could text Jess right now, and let her know she was on her way home!

Chloe's mum turned round to say something and saw Chloe busy texting. "You've only just said goodbye!" she laughed. "You can't need to communicate with each other already."

"I'm not texting Lolly," Chloe explained. "I'm just letting Jess know that I'm on my way home. Is it all right if I suggest we meet on Saturday?" she added, texting busily. "She doesn't break up from her school until Friday."

"Of course," her mum agreed with a smile. "Invite her round. It'll be good to see Jess again."

2 Long Days

The first couple of days of the holiday slipped by very quickly. It was lovely not to have to get up early every morning.

Because the weather was so warm, Chloe and her mum went to the outdoor pool with Ben on Friday. He was getting quite confident, much better than the last time Chloe had been with him.

"You're almost swimming!" Chloe said.

"I *am* swimming," he insisted, doing a very splashy doggie paddle while wearing his buoyancy aid.

"Well it's very good swimming for someone who's nearly five," said Chloe diplomatically.

When they got home they were famished, and Chloe

helped her mum make a bowl of pasta and a salad for dinner. Chloe was dressing the salad when her phone bleeped.

"It's Jess!" she said. "Can she come over at ten tomorrow? And then we'll go into town if that's okay."

"Can I come?" said Ben, who was standing on a chair next to Chloe, trying to help. "I want to see Jess too."

Chloe and her mum laughed. "Not this time, Benny," Chloe told him. "But maybe you'll see her when we come home again." She bent over and whispered in his ear. "I'm hoping Mum will let Jess stay for tea."

"Okay," Ben whispered back.

Chloe was dying to see Jess again. But when she turned up on the doorstep the next morning Chloe almost didn't recognize her.

"Your hair's *pink*!" she squealed. "It looks amazing. And you've had it cut shorter as well."

Jess grinned. "Well, it's good to see you too," she teased, tossing her glossy pink locks. "I did it last night to celebrate the end of term. It's not just you lot at Rockley Park who can look cool you know." She put on a silly expression and both girls collapsed into giggles.

"It looks brilliant," Chloe said once they'd both stopped laughing. "I wish I could try it. But my mum would have a fit if I did. And what about the county hockey team? Do they mind if their team members have pink hair? Congratulations by the way," she added hastily.

Jess had only just been picked to play hockey for the county; she hadn't had a chance to play for them yet.

"Thanks," said Jess with a grin. "And I'm not worried about whether it's allowed or not because the colour will have washed out by the time I go back to school. It's not a permanent dye, just a fun one for the summer."

Chloe looked admiringly at her friend's hair. Before she knew it she was giggling again, delighted to be with Jess after a whole term away.

"Come on," said Jess, nudging Chloe in the ribs. "Let's go into town."

It was great fun window-shopping together. And Chloe discovered that some things had altered since the last time she'd been home. Their favourite café had changed its name, and there was a new clothes shop in the high street, next to the music shop.

They had a look in the window. The clothes *were* pretty cool. There were several dresses Chloe could imagine Jess in, and a great pair of trousers that Chloe liked the look of.

"Let's go in," said Chloe, heading for the door. Jess followed.

They browsed the racks and found several things they both loved, but the prices were totally out of their range. Chloe headed over to a display of brightly coloured tops in the middle of the shop. "What d'you think, Jess?" she asked.

"I *love* the purple one," said Jess.

"Guess what?" Chloe grinned at her friend as soon as they left the shop. "I'm almost certain some of those tops are the same as the ones Lolly gave me on the last day of term. And one of them was purple. It'll go brilliantly with your pink hair! You've got to try it on when we get home."

Jess stared at her. "Really? Wow! Thanks, Chloe. It would be so cool if I could borrow it some time."

Chloe laughed. "There are *loads*. We can share them out between us and swap them about. It'll be fun!"

"Ooh, Chloe!" said Jess, looking thrilled. "Can we go back to yours now?"

Chloe laughed. "We haven't seen all the shops yet," she protested.

"Okay," agreed Jess, as they made their way down the street. "Let's get a sandwich for lunch. We could eat in the park. Chloe?"

Chloe was reading the handwritten adverts in the music shop window. They reminded her a bit of the noticeboard in the main hall at Rockley Park.

Bassist needed for a new project.
Heavy metal preferred.

Fender guitar for sale with practice amp.

*Drummer offers holiday-time lessons to
beginners or improvers.*

Chloe read the last advert again. "That's Danny!" she
said in surprise. "He's offering drum lessons."

"So?"

"Well," Chloe wasn't sure what she felt about it, "it's
just that it's interesting. He's on holiday from school,
and yet he's still busy with music. Good for him. I don't
suppose anyone would want singing lessons, would
they?" She sighed. "Anyway, I'd be hopeless at
teaching. I wonder if he has any takers yet?"

"Why don't you ask him?" suggested Jess. "Look,
he's in the shop."

Chloe peered through the glass. "Oh, yes! Come
on," she said, pushing at the door. "Let's go and
say hello."

3 A Terrible Shame

The shop door pinged as the girls went in but Danny was busy examining a drum kit and didn't notice them until they were right beside him.

"Hi!" said Chloe.

Danny jumped, and then grinned. "Hi!" he said. "Hello, Jess," he added. "I like your hair."

"Thanks!" she said, looking pleased.

"What are you up to?" asked Danny.

"Shopping," Chloe told him. "Then I saw your advert. Got any pupils yet?"

"I only just put the notice up!" he said.

"Well we're going to have a sandwich in the park," Chloe told him. "If you've finished drooling over those cymbals you could come with us if you like."

"Okay."

The three friends stopped at a shop to get some food, then they headed for the park. It was a lovely, sunny day, and loads of people were out enjoying themselves.

"Have you heard anything from the Rockley Park lot?" asked Chloe, screwing up her sandwich wrapper.

"I got a text from Marmalade," said Danny.

"That's your dancer friend, isn't it?" said Jess.

Danny nodded. "He said he's having a great time with all his younger sisters. I think they spoil him when he's home from school. And you know Marmalade, Chloe. He loves being the centre of attention."

"I wish I could meet him," said Jess. "He sounds fun."

"How about Ed and Ben?" asked Chloe. "Have you heard from them?"

"I think they're going abroad with their families some time over the summer."

"Well," said Chloe, throwing her rubbish in the bin next to them. "We're not going anywhere this year. But it's so great to see Jess again."

Jess smiled.

"In fact," Chloe went on. "Jess and I have some really important stuff to do this afternoon."

"We do?" said Jess, looking puzzled.

"Yes," said Chloe. "We ought to go. We have decisions to make about clothes."

Danny laughed. "Well have fun," he told them.

It didn't take long for the girls to get back home from the park. They ran up to Chloe's room and she took the pile of tops out of her wardrobe. Jess squealed with excitement.

"They *are* the same as the ones in the shop," she said, peering at the labels. "This is awesome!"

There were six tops, so they chose three each. The purple one *did* look fantastic on Jess, while the green one suited Chloe perfectly. Jess gave Chloe a big thank-you hug and then looked serious. "I have something I need to ask you," she said.

"What is it?" asked Chloe.

"The thing is," Jess looked awkward. "I know you don't have much space in your room."

Chloe looked puzzled. "I know. What's up, Jess?"

"It's just that…" Jess scowled. "My mum's got a new boyfriend, and they've booked a few days off early next month."

"But that's good, isn't it?" said Chloe. "She's been on her own for ages, hasn't she? Don't you like him? Is that it?"

Jess shook her head. "No. I do like him. He's great. Really nice." She twisted her lip. "But I don't want to go on holiday with them. I'd feel stupid, hanging around with them all the time. Mum needs to have fun without me getting in the way. So I wondered…"

Chloe smiled. "Of course you can come and stay here!" she said. "I'm sure Mum won't mind. Let's go and ask her in a minute. We can have a sleepover every night!"

✳

Chloe's mum and dad were very happy for Jess to stay. "As long as you don't mind sleeping on an air bed," Mum said.

"And being bounced on by Ben in the mornings," warned Chloe with a giggle.

"It's very thoughtful of you, Jessica," said Chloe's mum. "To give your mum some space. Write the dates on the calendar, Chloe. Then we won't forget."

Jess gave Chloe a big hug before she went home. "It's so brilliant that you're here again," she said. "I've got some good friends at my school, but we've been friends for *ever.* And that's special."

"It'll be special too, when you're camping on my floor," said Chloe. "I can't wait."

"Me neither," laughed Jess.

Chloe hardly had time to close the front door after Jess had gone when her mobile rang. It was Lolly!

"Hi! How are you?" said Chloe, going slowly back up to her room. "What are you up to?"

"We've got so much modelling work it's just not

true!" Lolly told her. "So much so that Mum said we can have a treat once it's finished."

"That sounds good," said Chloe, wondering what sort of treat the twins had in mind.

"It is!" said Lolly. "And you'll never guess what we asked for." She didn't give Chloe a chance to reply. "We're allowed to invite a friend each to come up to the London flat before our last show in the city, and then on to our house in Gloucestershire for a few days. Can you come, Chloe? I so hope you can."

"Wow!" Chloe had never been to a fashion show in London, and she hadn't been to the twins' country house or their city flat. It sounded fantastic.

"Pop's asking Tara, and I'm asking you," said Lolly. "Say you'll come."

"Of course I will," said Chloe at once. "I'm not going away or anything this summer so it'll be fine."

"Brilliant!" said Lolly. "Look I must go. I just wanted to tell you. Oh! Nearly forgot. The fashion show is on the fifth. See you very soon!"

"Lolly!" But Lolly had gone. Chloe bit her lip. Then

she slowly closed her phone and went back downstairs. She felt near to tears. She wanted to go and stay with Pop and Lolly, more than *anything*. But the date Lolly had given her was *impossible*.

4 A Problem to Solve

Chloe went into the kitchen and slumped down at the table. She was determined not to cry, but she could feel tears prickling the back of her eyes.

"Can you move?" her mum asked. "I need the table for a minute... Chloe?" she added, seeing her daughter's miserable face. "Whatever's the matter?"

"I thought this summer was going to be such fun," said Chloe. "But Lolly has just phoned to invite me to a fashion show and to stay with her afterwards, and it's when Jess is coming here!"

"Oh dear." Chloe's mum sat down beside her and put her arm around her. "These things happen," she said. "But you can't let Jess down."

"I know," agreed Chloe. "But it's such a shame."

Together they looked at the calendar, but there was no way Chloe could fit everything in. Jess was coming two days before the fashion show, and going three days afterwards.

Chloe felt distraught. "It was going to be me and my three roommates from school," she said. "It would have been so cool. And Pop and Lolly live in this mansion flat in London and have a *huge* house in the country. I've *never* had a chance to stay anywhere like that. Or go to a catwalk show in London. It's the chance of a lifetime. I may never get an opportunity to do this again." She looked at her mum. "But I can't let Jess down," she added miserably. "What am I going to do?"

"You can't go back on your word," her mum agreed. "You're right. It's a real shame, but I'm afraid you're going to have to say no to Lolly. It's a pity she rang off before you had a chance to tell her."

"It's my fault," said Chloe. "I told her it would be all right before she gave me the date."

"Don't blame yourself," her mum told her. "I'm sure

Lolly will understand when you explain that the date is no good."

"Maybe Tara will still be at Pop and Lolly's when Jess goes home," said Chloe in a sudden rush of hopefulness. "Perhaps I could join them for the last day or so." But Chloe was clutching at straws, and she knew it. It wouldn't be the same if she turned up at the last minute. Besides, Lolly would invite someone else. Chloe couldn't expect her to be on her own if Pop had Tara as her guest. No. Chloe just couldn't go. It was as simple as that.

"It's late now," she mumbled to her mum. "I'll phone Lolly in the morning."

"All right," said Mrs. Tompkins sympathetically. "But don't leave it too late for her to invite someone else."

Chloe knew her mum was right, but the comment made her feel even more miserable.

Chloe went upstairs and sat on her bed. She really ought to phone Lolly now. It wasn't fair to let her think she'd got everything sorted out, when she hadn't at all. Chloe's fingers hovered over the phone keys, but she simply couldn't bring herself to call the number. She found herself scrolling through her contacts list and stopping at Jess's number instead. Her fingers flew over the keys as she tapped out a text.

Did you tell your mum about staying with me?

She closed her eyes and pressed send. Maybe, just maybe Jess had told her mum, and her mum really, really wanted Jess to go with them. Maybe it was all a big misunderstanding and tomorrow Jess would ring to say that she wouldn't be sleeping on Chloe's floor after all. How terrible it would be if Chloe had turned down Lolly's invitation, only to find that the arrangement with Jess was off!

Chloe couldn't settle to anything for the rest of the evening. She plugged in her phone, even though it didn't really need charging, and kept willing it to bleep. Several times she almost rang Jess, but she didn't want to hound her for an answer.

Eventually, just as she had decided to go to bed, her phone rang. Chloe grabbed it and flipped it open. It was Jess.

"Oh, Chloe!" Jess said, without even saying hello. "Mum's so pleased I'm coming to you! I mean, she tried to insist I went away with her and David, but I could tell she was just trying to be nice. Honestly, she's like a little kid now! It's so long since she's been anywhere, and she's so excited. And David said he'd give me some money for us both to go to the cinema, so we get a bit of a treat as well. They're both downstairs now, looking up last-minute hotel deals on the internet. Isn't it great when it's so easy to make people happy!"

Chloe made her voice sound as pleased as possible. And she *was* pleased for Jess and her mum. "Well, that's all settled then," she said.

Jess didn't notice how flat Chloe's voice sounded. "Anyway, I must go," she told Chloe. "Mum's yelling at me to get to bed! Thanks for everything, Chloe. See you very soon!"

Chloe closed her phone and put it on her bed. So that was that. No fashion show, no joining in with her Rockley Park friends. However hard she tried she couldn't help feeling sad. She told herself how lucky she was to have so many good friends that she had to turn invitations down, but she was still wistful.

It was late, but she decided to phone Lolly anyway. If she left it until the morning she might find it even harder to turn down the invitation. Once the decision was made she could concentrate on having a good time with Jess.

Lolly almost always picked up straight away, and this time was no exception. "Chloe!" she said. "I wondered who was calling so late."

"Sorry," said Chloe.

"Don't be," Lolly told her. "I hadn't gone to bed. I was just thinking I ought to."

"Me too," said Chloe.

"Anyway, what do you want?" said Lolly cheerfully.

"It's about me coming to stay," said Chloe wretchedly. "I'm afraid I can't."

Lolly sounded shocked. "Oh no! Why not?" she said. "I thought it was a done deal. If your parents are concerned about you being in London I'm sure

Mum would speak to them about it and reassure them."

"It's not that," said Chloe.

Lolly listened as Chloe explained about Jess and her mum. "Oh dear," she said when Chloe had finished. "I can see your problem. Of course you can't let Jess down. That would be awful."

"Yes," agreed Chloe in a small voice.

"But look, there will be other times," continued Lolly. "Don't be too sad about it. It's not London Fashion Week or anything really exciting, just a big London store putting on a show. And as for afterwards, well, we'll be back together again in September anyway."

"I'm sorry to let you down," said Chloe. "I really wanted to come."

Lolly sounded sorry too. "I know," she said. "But cheer up, or you'll have me in tears."

Chloe tried to laugh, but she was near to tears herself. "Well have a good time," she said, swallowing hard.

"And you," said Lolly. "Enjoy being with Jess. I know

she's always been a special friend for you. See you at the end of the summer."

Chloe put her phone down. She knew she'd done the right thing, but it was very hard. If only the dates hadn't clashed. She could have helped Jess out *and* gone to stay with Lolly too. Oh well, it was done now, and it really was time for bed.

5 Tara Time

Like Pop and Lolly, Tara Fitzgerald was in London. She was happy *not* to be involved with fashion shows, even though her mother was a fashion journalist. Just now, her mum was in Poland, researching an article for her magazine and, while she was away, Tara was having a wonderful time with her father, Fitz, who was a session musician.

At last she had convinced him that she was old enough to go with him when he worked in a recording studio. Up until now he'd insisted that the long hours and need for quiet during recording would bore his only daughter.

But Tara had been at Rockley Park school for two

years now, and she had experience of working in the school's studio. Her father couldn't pretend that she wasn't grown up enough to be sensible these days! And there was another reason for her to spend time with him there. Fitz had promised that she could play with him at his jazz club. With such long hours in the studio it was hard for Tara and her dad to find the time to practise. As soon as they got home all Fitz wanted was a meal and some sleep. But there were regular breaks at the studio, and he aimed to fit in a bit of practice with Tara then.

Tara was in the control room, while her father was in the glass-walled studio. He had been recording some music for a TV drama and was listening to a playback of the latest recording. When it was finished he nodded. "How does that sound to you?" he asked.

His words were picked up by a microphone in the soundproofed room, so everyone in the control room could hear what he said.

"I think that's one to keep, Fitz," said John, the engineer. "Do you want to come through while I have a

sort out here? Maybe Tara will put the kettle on for us."
He turned to Tara and grinned. He liked to tease her,
while she was at pains to make it obvious that she
wasn't an unpaid tea lady.

"How long until you're ready?" asked Fitz.

"Say twenty minutes tops? I need to make a couple
of phone calls too."

"Okay. Tara, do you fancy coming through for a
quick practice?"

"Sure!" Tara replied, speaking to her father through
the control room microphone.

The lighting in the control room was quite muted,
and the walls and floor were both covered in dark
purple carpet, but the studio was a blaze of light. Tara's
lovely, black-and-white Rickenbacker bass guitar was
already in there, on a stand next to the grand piano.
She went in and picked it up.

"Okay?" asked her father.

Tara gave him a grin.

"Right then. Shall we run through *Scattered
Lives* again?"

"Do you think we'll be good enough to play it by Tuesday?" Tara asked.

"No probs," said her father cheerfully. "We'll be more than ready. And I want my friend Bix Klieder to hear your latest piece. I reckon he'll be really impressed that I've got such a talented daughter."

Tara smiled. It meant a lot to her that she should be taken seriously as a songwriter as well as a musician. In fact, she wanted to make a career out of writing songs if she could.

They picked up their instruments. Soon, Fitz's bluesy saxophone rose above Tara's bass. She had to admit it, her father really made her music soar.

"Maybe you're right," she admitted when the piece came to an end. "Perhaps we will be ready."

"Of course we will," Fitz told her, with a smile. "Now. I'd better have a few minutes' rest before I start the next session. You know, you ought to finish writing some lyrics for *Scattered Lives*," he added as she put her bass back on its rest. "Then, you never know, Bix might sing them with us some time."

"Really?"

Fitz came out of the studio with his daughter and headed for the little kitchen next to the control room. "You never know," he said. "He might even sing them on Tuesday if you have them ready by then. He only has to listen to a tune once to get it into his head. If you print the lyrics out and hand them to him he won't be able to resist. By the way, did you put the kettle on?"

Tara scowled at him and he laughed.

She went back to her corner in the control room and pulled a scruffy notebook out of her back pocket. She had a wonderful leather-bound notebook at home, which famous chat show host Sebastian Walters had given her a while ago, but she used that for copying up her finished songs. The scruffy notebook was for working out ideas.

Tara had been thinking about writing the lyrics, and already had a few lines jotted down, but nothing was quite right. She read over what she'd done so far and frowned. If Bix Klieder might sing she needed to come up with some good lyrics pretty soon. He was a well-respected jazz drummer and singer, and he wouldn't be impressed by anything other than her very best efforts.

Fitz was back in the studio now. They would be recording the last piece for the drama next. It was by far the longest piece, and he'd said it was tricky to get right. Tara had plenty of time to work on her song. She took the cap off her pen and stared into space. If she let her mind run free she would come up with something good. She usually did.

By the time Tuesday night came around Tara was feeling quite nervous. She was used to playing in public, but her father's jazz club was out of her comfort zone. There would be no other teenagers there, and she usually played rock, not jazz. Fitz told her to stay cool.

"I've been going to this club for years," he said. "Tuesday night is open-mike night. Whoever turns up gets to play, and it's very chilled. It's just a night for jamming together and having fun. So relax. With your experience and ability you really don't need to worry."

Tara waited on the pavement with their instrument cases as Fitz paid off the taxi.

"Come on then, sweetie. This way."

He led Tara along a dingy alley and down some badly lit stairs. At the bottom was a blank door. It didn't look as if anything happened down here. But her father pushed it open, and Tara saw a narrow corridor stretching ahead of them. It wasn't easy, carrying the awkward cases along the corridor, especially when a huge man came out of a side door and they had to squeeze past.

"This your daughter, Fitz?" the big man asked, smiling at Tara.

"Sure is," agreed Fitz. "Meet Tara."

"I'm Bix Klieder, one of your dad's buddies." He offered his hand and Tara shook it.

"She's got something for you." Fitz gave her a nudge, and Tara pulled the words of her song out of her pocket.

"What's this?" asked Bix with a smile.

"Dad thought you might like to read the lyrics to

Scattered Lives, the song we're doing tonight," said Tara diffidently.

"Wow! Thanks, Tara. I'll be sure to read them over before your slot. Catch you later."

Somehow Tara had imagined Bix Klieder to be slightly built and intense, with dark glasses and a nerdy jacket, not this larger-than-life figure with a broad grin. He was so much less scary than she had feared.

Tara and her father found a seat in the dimly lit room. The lighting was so low it took a while for Tara to get her bearings, especially as people kept coming up to say hello. But everyone was very friendly, and treated her as though she belonged. She was here for the music, and that made her one of them.

By the time their turn came to get up on the tiny stage Tara was feeling quite relaxed. Bix seemed to be in charge of the proceedings, and she felt safe with him, squeezed as he was behind his drum kit for their number. And she was thrilled to have her father by her side.

"This here is Tara Fitzgerald, folks," said Bix into

his microphone. "Come to play us her new song, *Scattered Lives*. Her dad already knows it so he's gonna play along. I got some words here, but we'll see how we do. Okay, doll?" he added, giving her a big wink.

Tara nodded, trying not to laugh. She'd never been called "doll" before. She hitched her guitar strap over her head, looked at her father, and when he was ready she began.

After the first few bars, Bix started to use his brushes to give a gentle, sweeping, background rhythm, and when it came to the second verse he started singing the odd line in a fantastically rich voice. Tara almost wanted to stop playing so she could listen to him properly, but the song was only halfway through. She had to carry on.

Before it came to an end a couple of guitarists got up with their instruments and added some welcome top notes to Fitz's sax. A woman Tara hadn't noticed before joined her voice with Bix's; without words, she just let her voice soar through and around the tune.

When the jam session eventually came to an end, Tara was totally blown away. "Can we come next Tuesday?" she asked her father in the cab, heading back home.

He laughed. "So you liked it then?"

"Of course!" said Tara with a happy sigh. "It was wonderful."

"Well we can't go next week," he told her. "Remember? I have to be in Seattle for a recording. Your mum will be home by then but this isn't her scene. She won't want to take you. We can go later in the holiday if you like."

"Okay."

Tara reached into her pocket and pulled out her phone. Someone had texted her. And she had three missed calls, all from her Rockley Park school friend, Pop. The text was from Pop as well. Tara read it and laughed.

Can you come to a catwalk show next week (not too long) and then to stay over in the country for a bit? Popxxxxx

Tara's fingers flew over her phone keys.

You must be joking! I couldn't bear a fashion show. I'd love to come and stay over though. When next week?

She grinned at her father.

"Pop's gone mad," she told him. "She's just invited me to a fashion show, and to stay over next week."

Her father laughed.

"Can you give the show a miss and still see her?" he asked. "Or would that be rude? Your mum and I are going to the Lowthers' summer party at the end of next week. I wonder if you'd be allowed to stay with Pop until after that? If so, we could all go home together afterwards?"

"I'll find out," said Tara. "Pop knows I hate fussing about clothes, so I don't suppose she'll mind too much if I miss the show. I'll speak to her tomorrow and find out."

It would be a laugh to go and stay with Pop. By all accounts the Lowther twins' house in the country was huge, with lots of land. It would be great to get out into the countryside for a few days and fun to spend some time with her best friend, Pop. Tara couldn't wait to catch up. And if her dad was going to be in Seattle for a day or two there would be no more jamming for a while. Yes, staying with Pop was just what she needed.

6 Pop's Good Idea

"Oh, knicker elastic!"

A long-suffering dresser was waiting with the next dress, but Pop was reading a message on her phone.

"Pop!" hissed Lolly. Her sister wasn't being very professional. Lolly was far too polite to keep anyone hanging about. Okay, so this was a photo shoot, not a frenetic, catwalk show, where every second counted, but Simon Birdstock was a very expensive photographer, and the editor of *Glossy Pages*, the magazine that had commissioned the shots, would be really annoyed if they held him up.

Pop threw her phone onto the make-up table and raised her arms. The dresser dropped the scarlet dress over Pop's head, and she disappeared in a froth of frilled silk.

When her beautifully made-up face appeared again she was scowling.

"Knicker elastic!"

"You already said that," Lolly told her, as she was buttoned into a dress identical to her sister's. "What's the problem?"

"The problem…" exclaimed Pop dramatically.

Pop's dresser rolled her eyes, and Lolly stifled a giggle. The last thing Pop needed was encouragement. "Is what?"

"It's Tara," said Pop, looking suddenly as deflated as a burst balloon. "She's not coming to the fashion show either."

She held still while the make-up artist applied more lipgloss.

"What a shame," said Lolly. "We're not having much luck with our friends, are we? No Chloe and no Tara. It's a real pity. Mind you, I thought you were asking a bit much, expecting Tara, of all people, to come to a fashion show. She'd hate it!" Lolly sighed. "We'll just have to ask Aunt Aggie and Uncle Eric if they'd like the tickets. They live close enough to get to the store under their own steam."

"No way!" said Pop. "The last time we invited them Aunt Aggie spent the entire show glowering at me."

There was no time for Lolly to reply. They were ready, and Simon Birdstock was already tapping his foot impatiently. The twins hurried onto the set and arranged themselves in front of a backdrop of a wedding reception. At once, Pop assumed a vibrant expression. Her eyes sparkled under the bright lights and she looked for all the world as if she was at an exciting event.

Lolly did the same. They complied as the stylist moved them about and tried different accessories with their outfits. When the stylist was happy it was Simon's turn.

"Look at me, both of you. Lovely! Now have a conversation. Come on, this is the event of the year for you. You can't believe you're there. Okay, turn a fraction to your left, Lolly. No, sorry I mean Pop. "

He took hundreds of photographs, and had to change the memory card in his camera several times.

"Now you are two of the most beautiful people at the reception. I want confidence, gloss, glamour."

Lolly gave Pop a highly superior smile, and Pop responded by raising her eyebrows a touch. It was perfectly done.

"And relax," said Simon, putting one camera down and picking up another. "I'll do some black and white too. Okay, let's pick it up again."

"That wasn't much of a relax," said Pop out of the corner of her mouth.

"Don't do that," complained Simon. "You're not a gangster, Pop."

Lolly tried to think of something else, anything other than her sister playing the fool. If she wasn't careful she'd get the giggles, and she knew from past experience how difficult it was to model successfully if you kept laughing.

Pop's Good Idea

A few minutes later they went back into the dressing room for their last change of clothes. This time it was linen trousers and matching jackets.

"I've had an idea," said Pop, stepping into the wide-legged, cream-coloured trousers.

"You're going to start behaving at photo shoots?" hazarded Lolly. She slipped elegantly into hers, and with her dresser's help, shrugged on the close-fitting jacket. Then she slipped her feet into a gorgeous pair of shoes and waited patiently, while her dresser did them up.

"Any colour, as long as it's beige!" said Pop, looking at them both in the full-length mirror.

"Cream and taupe, actually," said her sister tartly. "And the theme is 'Colours to take you from smart to casual and beyond', according to the brief. So what is your idea?" But Pop couldn't reply because the make-up artist was there again with the lipgloss.

Back on set, a huge Harley-Davidson motorbike had magically appeared under the lights.

"I didn't hear that arriving," said Lolly in surprise.

"Well I don't suppose they revved it up and rode it into the studio!" Pop said with a laugh. "I expect they just wheeled it in." She looked at the gleaming machine critically. "Does the brief tell us if this is supposed to represent smart, casual or beyond?"

Lolly stifled a giggle. "Beyond, probably," she suggested.

The stylist handed Pop a helmet and put a pair of gauntlets on the bike's tank. "Drape your right arm casually there," she explained. "The magazine wants a carefree look for this picture. That's it. Now, Lolly, you come and stand round the other side, with your hands on the handlebars, as if you're tempted to jump on and ride away."

"But she's got the helmet," protested Lolly.

"It doesn't have to be accurate," the stylist told her huffily. "It just has to be photogenic."

Pop couldn't wait for the stylist to leave so she could tell Lolly her idea. "We could invite Chloe's friend...what's her name, Jess, to the fashion show. Then Chloe could come too."

Lolly stared at her.

"Okay, girls," said Simon. "Ready for the last session?"

It was a while before the twins could continue their conversation, and they had to concentrate on what they were doing during the shoot. There wasn't any time for Lolly to think about what Pop had said. But as soon as they had finished, and were getting back into their own clothes, Lolly spoke.

"If I invited both Chloe and Jess you wouldn't have a friend coming," she said. "It's really nice of you, Pop, but it wouldn't be fair."

Pop grinned. "Tara's going to come and stay," she told Lolly. "It's just the show she's passing on. So don't worry about that."

Lolly still looked worried. "But we don't know Jess," she protested. "Well, only what Chloe has told us about her. Would Mum let us invite a stranger, and would *Jess's* mum let her come?"

Pop shrugged. "We won't know unless we ask," she said. "But Jess is a friend of Chloe's. She can't be *totally* awful. She's probably really nice. At least she'd be better than Aunt Aggie!"

For a moment Lolly looked undecided. Then her face cleared and she grinned. "Okay," she agreed. "Good idea, Pop. Let's go for it."

7 A New Plan

Chloe was in the garden with Ben when her phone rang. They were creating a whole world in his sandpit, with plastic animals in the "fields" and lots of wiggly roads.

She was expecting a call from Jess, and when she saw it was from Lolly she was surprised.

"Are you all right?" asked Lolly.

"Fine," lied Chloe. "I'm playing with Ben in his sandpit."

"Sweet," said Lolly.

"Anyway. How are you?" asked Chloe.

"Really good. We did a photo shoot for *Glossy Pages* magazine yesterday. I had to pretend I was just about to jump on a huge motorbike. I was a bit scared it might fall over and crush us, but I didn't dare say anything!"

Chloe found herself laughing. It was good talking to Lolly again.

"But that's not why I phoned," continued Lolly. "I've got an idea for you, and I'd like to know what you think."

"What is it?" asked Chloe, holding the phone with one hand and placing a three-legged sheep firmly into the sand so it didn't fall over.

"Well, Pop asked Tara to the fashion show," said Lolly. "But of course she doesn't want to come. So we still have two spare tickets. We wondered if you would like to come…and bring Jess too? …Chloe? Are you still there?"

"Yes," said Chloe, in a daze. "I don't know what to say."

"It doesn't matter if you don't want to," said Lolly. "But it was having Jess with you that meant you couldn't come in the first place. We just thought it might be an answer. Is it the sort of thing she'd be interested in?"

"Of *course* it is," said Chloe with rising excitement. "She'd absolutely love it. She's really into clothes. And you'll never guess what. She's dyed her hair bright pink for the holidays!"

"Cool!" said Lolly. "When Pop sees it she'll want to do the same!"

"I'm not sure how we'd get up to London and back in a day," Chloe mused, trying to think sensibly.

"But it wouldn't just be one day," Lolly told her. "If you came up by coach the day before, we'd meet you at the coach station. You'd stay the first night in our London flat and we'd go down to Gloucestershire after the show. We'd have to sort your return journey out, but there's a good train service from the nearest town."

"You mean...both of us could *stay* as well?" Chloe couldn't believe her ears. "But you don't even know Jess!"

"That doesn't matter," said Lolly. "She's got to be nice if she's your friend! And we'll do our best to make sure she doesn't feel left out. After all, we're on holiday. We won't be talking about school all the time."

Chloe knew how good Lolly was at making people feel welcome. She'd been so friendly on that first day at school. Chloe had been rather overawed at finding that she would be sharing a room with two famous models but Lolly had soon put her at ease.

"What about Pop?" said Chloe. "She won't have a friend. If Tara doesn't go and Jess and I do it's not fair on her."

Lolly laughed. "I said that too," she told Chloe. "But Tara is coming down to the house with us. It's just the fashion show she's avoiding. It'll be fun. Please come."

Chloe felt her heart leap. Of course she wanted to go. But it would have to be agreed by Jess, and Jess's mum as well as her own. She was determined not to get too excited until she knew it was okay. It was bad enough being disappointed the first time. It would be too cruel if she had to turn down the invitation for a second time.

"I'll have to ask," she said soberly. "And so will Jess.

I'll let you know as soon as I can. Thanks ever so much, Lolly. And thank Pop for me too."

"I will," said Lolly. "And I'll keep my fingers crossed. I do hope you can make it."

"So do I," agreed Chloe, trying to curb her excitement. "Oh, Lolly, so do I!"

Chloe brushed the sand from her clothes and went to look for her mum. She walked into her mother's workroom and watched, while her mum ran a seam down a great swathe of green, patterned fabric. Chloe's mum worked from home. She was making curtains for a customer.

"Is Ben all right?" her mum asked as soon as she had finished the seam.

Chloe nodded. "We're in the sandpit," she said.

"Well don't track sand in here, Chloe. This machine doesn't like grit in it. And if the fabric gets dirty I'll be paying for dry-cleaning."

"Okay." Chloe stayed where she was, and leaned against the door. It didn't take long to explain Lolly's idea.

"*If* Jess is keen, and *if* her mother agrees, you can

go," said Chloe's mum. "But you won't try to bully Jess into going, will you? Let her make up her own mind."

"Of course I will," Chloe agreed.

Chloe went back into the garden with a smile on her face. Her mum was always the hardest person to convince about anything Chloe wanted to do. The only person she had to convince now was Jess, and surely she'd think it was a *brilliant* idea.

Ben had got fed up with the sandpit, and was riding on his lorry instead, so Chloe sat in the swing seat, opened her phone and rang Jess.

She explained the situation and then held her breath, waiting to see what Jess would say. For a moment there was silence, and then Jess yelled down the phone.

"Pop and Lolly Lowther! Are you serious?"

"Of course I'm serious." Chloe grinned to herself. It would be all right. Jess was even more excited than she was.

As expected, Jess's mum was okay with the idea. But there was a lot to do in the couple of days they had before they left for London. Both girls needed clothes washed, and they were both in agony about what to wear to the fashion show.

"It's got to be a really fashionable dress, and totally on trend," said Jess, sounding like one of the fashion magazines she was so fond of reading. "And the bad news is that I don't have anything like that."

"And shoes!" squeaked Chloe, eyeing her feet with dismay. "My only smart shoes are vile!"

Thanks to Jess's mum, they soon calmed down. "No one will be looking at you," she said. "It would be very nice if you had expensive designer clothes, but you don't. So don't compete if you can't win. Just wear something smart and you'll feel fine. Other people will be in the same boat."

After a busy time washing and ironing clothes, Chloe's mum sent her into town to buy a present for Pop and Lolly's mum.

"Go to that new chocolate shop," she suggested, giving Chloe some money. "And don't buy anything too ordinary. Something small, but delicious, ought to do the trick. You have to take a little something to thank her for having you both."

"I'd rather have a big bag of sweets from the corner shop," Jess whispered to Chloe, as they peered at the display of French, Belgian and Italian confectionery in the window.

In the end they chose champagne truffles. They looked very sophisticated, nestling in a small gold box and tied up with golden ribbon.

Back home Chloe put the box of truffles carefully into her bag. Now they were packed and ready to go. All they had to do was catch the London bus.

8 Meeting the Lowthers

Chloe's mum took the girls to the coach station.

"Make sure you text me as soon as you're met at the other end," she told Chloe as they got on the bus. "And if they're not there don't wander off."

"Mu-um!" said Chloe. "We're not stupid. I've got Lolly's number. If they've been held up she'll phone me, so we'll be fine. Don't worry."

The girls waved through the window as the bus pulled out of the station. As soon as it turned onto the road they exchanged glances and giggled excitedly.

"I can't believe I'm going to a real, live London fashion show," said Jess, her eyes shining. Then she looked a bit worried. "I hope Pop and Lolly like me."

"Of course they will," said Chloe confidently. "They're very easy to get on with. I just hope *you* like *them.*"

"Well I'm pretty easy to get on with, aren't I?" asked Jess.

Chloe nodded.

"Well then," said Jess happily, relaxing into her seat. "I expect we'll *all* get on fine."

Pop and Lolly were both waiting at the bus station when Chloe and Jess arrived. The twins were dressed in jeans and T-shirts, and anxiously scanning the crowd of passengers. As soon as they saw Chloe they started waving wildly.

"Hi! It's great to see you," said Lolly, giving Chloe a big hug.

"And you're Jess, right?" said Pop. "Good to meet you. I'm so glad you could come. Wow! I *love* your hair!" Both twins gave Jess a quick hug too, and Chloe noticed that she went pink with pleasure.

"Let's hurry," said Lolly. "The car is on a double yellow line."

As soon as they'd retrieved the luggage from the bus, they all headed out of the station. Sure enough, a large car was waiting in a restricted zone. Pop put their bags in the boot and then wrenched the back door open. Chloe and Jess piled in, followed by Lolly. Pop got into the front passenger seat and the car drove off.

"Sorry I wasn't able to say hello properly, but I didn't want to get a parking ticket," the woman who was driving apologized. "I'm Leela Lowther, Poppy and Polly's mother."

Pop turned round to look at Chloe and Jess. She grimaced at her mother's use of the twins' full names and Lolly poked her arm to make her behave.

"Pleased to meet you," said Chloe. "It's really kind of you to have us to stay," she added politely.

"Not at all," said Mrs. Lowther.

Chloe looked at Jess to make sure she was all right. Jess raised her eyebrows and grinned, stroking the soft leather seat they were sitting on.

"So, where's the fashion show?" asked Chloe, turning to Lolly.

"It's at Plumley's," Lolly said.

"A huge department store," added Pop.

"They put one on every season," explained Lolly. "We're going to model the clothes they'll be selling in the autumn."

"It would be so cool if you could come to a show during British Fashion Week," said Pop. "But tickets are like gold dust."

"We thought this would be fun anyway," added Lolly. "It's a bit more relaxed."

They soon arrived at the Lowther's apartment. It was in a very smart part of town, and had an underground car park with a lift to take them up to their flat.

The twins showed Chloe and Jess to their room. It was quite small, but had a stunning view from the window.

"This is great! Thank you," said Jess, putting her case down. "Do you stay here often?"

Pop smiled. "Yes. This apartment is so convenient when we're working, but we try to spend as much of the summer as we can in the country," she said. "It's much more relaxing. Do you like swimming? We've got a pool there, which is great for cooling off when it's hot. I'm not a brilliant swimmer, but I do like messing about in the water."

"Me too," said Jess.

Chloe and Lolly smiled at each other. Jess and Pop seemed to be hitting it off really well, thank goodness.

Because the twins were working the next day they had to have an early night. "We'll be in trouble if we turn up with bags under our eyes," explained Pop. "But as soon as we've finished work we'll be able to stay up later."

"In fact we'll probably sit up half the night chatting," giggled Lolly.

When the twins went to bed Chloe and Jess did too. They were sharing a room, and as they didn't need to worry so much about their beauty sleep, the early night was an opportunity to chat.

"They are *so* nice," sighed Jess contentedly. "And Pop's a real giggle, isn't she?"

"I'm glad you like them," said Chloe with relief. "They certainly seem to like you."

"I thought they'd be all stuck up, and speak with posh accents," said Jess. "But they aren't like that at all."

"I *told* you," said Chloe.

"Their mum is very posh though," said Jess. "I don't know if she approves of me or not. She's *so* polite."

"Me neither," agreed Chloe. "And this flat is so *smart.* If Pop and Lolly weren't here, leaving things lying around, I'd be scared to touch anything!"

"I suppose it's so totally normal for them, having such nice things, that they don't notice," mused Jess.

"Imagine what their other house must be like," said Chloe, getting into bed.

"I expect it's like a *palace*," giggled Jess.

Chloe sank into the fragrant cotton sheets and plump pillows. The bedding was a crisp white, including the duvet cover, and it all felt wonderfully luxurious. "Looking forward to tomorrow?" she asked Jess.

"Mmm," replied Jess from her bed. "If I can bring myself to get out of this bed in the morning!"

Chloe laughed. "I know what you mean," she said.

"And I've changed my mind about what to wear," Jess went on.

"Have you?" Chloe looked at her best dress, hanging up on the wardrobe door. She'd bought a new pair of strappy sandals to go with it and was rather pleased with her outfit. "Aren't you wearing your dress then?"

"No." Jess looked over at Chloe. "I brought my black skirt with me. And I think I'll wear one of the tops you gave me. They're the best clothes I've got, and they're really trendy. Why don't you wear one too?"

"Because I like my dress," Chloe told her. "I'm keeping the tops for when we're at the house in the country."

"Fair enough," said Jess, burrowing deep down under her duvet. "Night then."

"Night."

9 Fantastic Fashion Show

The girls had to be up early, to make sure that the twins got to the fashion show in good time. When Jess came in for breakfast, she was wearing the purple top that Chloe had passed on to her from Lolly. Pop spotted it right away.

"Wow!" she said appreciatively. "You've got good taste, Jess. We love that designer's work. In fact they sent us their whole range of tops just before the end of term." She laughed. "Lolly gave some to Chloe because Mum was having a fit over all our luggage."

Jess looked awkward, but Lolly came to her rescue. "And that's one of them, isn't it?" she exclaimed. "What a great idea, Chloe, to share them. Jess, you look gorgeous! That colour is perfect with your hair."

But there wasn't much time to chat. They had to get to Plumley's, and the London traffic was terrible. Although they set out really early the twins were getting quite anxious by the time the car reached the back of the store.

Once they'd managed to park, they all got out, and went with Pop and Lolly to the third floor, where the fashion show was going to be. The twins said a hasty goodbye.

"See you later," said Lolly. "I hope you enjoy the show."

As the twins disappeared backstage, Mrs. Lowther relaxed. "Well, we have some time to kill before the show starts," she told Chloe and Jess. "I'm giving a large party in a few days' time, so I have an appointment with my personal shopper. She promised she'd find me something to wear. You can either come with me or have a look around the store by yourselves, as long as you promise not to go outside."

Jess and Chloe looked at each other. "Could we

have a look around here?" asked Chloe. "There's so much to see. We won't leave the building."

Jess nodded fiercely. "We promise," she said.

Mrs. Lowther looked at the girls. "Well, I can't imagine watching me trying on clothes would be much fun for you," she admitted. "I tell you what though. Just a moment." She rummaged in her handbag and brought out several vouchers. "I don't suppose you could use any of these, could you? I get sent them all the time and never remember to use them." She peered at the top one. "I think they're still valid."

"Oh we couldn't possibly," said Chloe politely, wondering what the vouchers were for.

"Of course you could," said Mrs. Lowther. "Go on. Take them, but make sure you're back for the show. Here, I'll give you your tickets as well. Don't lose them!"

"We won't," said Jess. "And thank you so much for the vouchers!"

"You're very welcome," said Mrs. Lowther. "Now I must go or I'll be late. See you at eleven fifteen on the third floor."

With that she disappeared in the direction of the lift, and Jess and Chloe exchanged looks. *"I can't imagine watching me trying on clothes would be much fun,"* Jess mimicked before bursting into laughter.

"Jess, don't!" said Chloe. "She's been really kind to us." But Chloe was giggling too, however hard she tried not to. It would have been terribly embarrassing watching someone else's mum trying on clothes, not to mention totally boring.

Jess and Chloe examined the vouchers. They were all valid for use in Plumley's, but most of them were quite specific. "'Ten pounds off Age-Defying Cream'," said Chloe. "I don't think we'll need that one!"

Jess looked at another. "'Free beach bag with any Cruiseline swimsuit'," she read. "I could do with a swimsuit, but I bet they're really dire. It sounds as if they're for old people."

"Let's go and find this place," suggested Chloe. "There's fifteen pounds off any purchase in Plumley's Boutique in the Basement."

The lifts were all busy, so the girls went down the

escalator. The boutique had just their style of clothes, even though they were rather expensive. But there was a sale on, and the friends spent ages looking for bargains. They had a few pounds of their own to spend. With careful searching of the sale items they eventually found a shiny black belt that Chloe loved, and a sparkly bag that Jess really wanted. With the fifteen pounds off from the voucher, they could just afford them, so they took their purchases to the till and presented their voucher. The woman at the till rang up the reduced amount and smiled at them. "You've got a good eye for a bargain," she said.

"Thank you," said Jess, taking the bag.

"I ought to get my mum something," said Chloe as they waited for the lift.

"Let's go up to the ground floor then," suggested Jess, examining the list of departments on the wall nearby. "There's souvenirs there. We might be able to find something."

They walked up, reached the foyer, and stared out through the glass doors at the hordes of people rushing by on the pavement outside. Chloe watched several red buses and a couple of black taxis in amongst the traffic. It was so busy she didn't feel at all tempted to go outside.

"This notebook and pen would be good for Mum," she told Jess after looking for a while. "We need a new one for phone messages."

"And I'll get my mum this mug," said Jess. "We're always breaking them in our house."

It was almost time for the fashion show, so the girls hurried into a lift. Lots of other people were going to the third floor as well, so it was quite a squeeze. And when they got there, they found themselves at the end of a large queue. When they finally got to the entrance, they handed in their tickets and were shown to their seats.

"We're in the front row!" Jess whispered to Chloe excitedly, as they sat down.

They were halfway down one side of the catwalk, and if they'd reached out they could almost have touched it. It was a great position. Chloe glanced around to see what everyone else was wearing. She was reassured to see that there were loads of different styles, and she didn't feel out of place at all.

After a few minutes, Mrs. Lowther turned up, looking very relieved to see them. "I had a fit of the horrors after we'd split up," she confided. "I don't know what I'd have said to your parents if I'd lost you, but you're obviously both very sensible girls. Did you find any of the vouchers useful?"

"Yes! Thanks ever so much," Chloe said. "We both found something in the Boutique in the Basement."

"Well done," said Mrs. Lowther.

"Do you want the vouchers back that we didn't use?" asked Jess.

Mrs. Lowther shook her head. "No," she said. "I'll never get round to using them. I'm hopeless with things like that." She laughed, and Chloe found herself warming a bit more to Pop and Lolly's mum. She could see that Mrs. Lowther was quite a nice person, although Chloe was sure she would always feel the need to be on her best behaviour while they were with her.

As soon as everyone had taken their seats, a blaze of spotlights lit the catwalk. Loud music began, and the lights pulsed in time to the beat. The show was about to begin!

The first few models were adults, but then they started showing clothes from the Boutique in the Basement. Jess gave Chloe a nudge when Pop and Lolly appeared, looking fantastic in shorts and flowing tops. They strode down the catwalk together, turning and pausing, and passing each other a couple of times, before continuing on their way to the end. There they paused for a bit longer, showing off the stylish look before striding back up the catwalk. A few minutes later they appeared again, wearing skirts and tops. As Pop shimmied past them she gave Jess and Chloe a big grin.

Mrs. Lowther tutted at her daughter's behaviour, and Chloe had to suppress a smile.

The show was over far too quickly. It had been wonderful seeing the clothes, and exciting to be a guest in the front row, but most of all it had been amazing to see Pop and Lolly performing so brilliantly on the catwalk.

When the lights went up, Mrs. Lowther chatted with several people in the audience. It seemed she knew quite a few of them, and they all wanted to compliment her on her daughters' performances. No one took any notice of Chloe and Jess, so they were able to soak up the atmosphere.

"Isn't that Keira Konner from that new girl band?" asked Jess. She pointed to a couple walking away from the fashion show. Keira was carrying a toddler dressed in designer jeans, top and shoes.

"Oh yes!" said Chloe. "That's her baby, Dynamo. What a name!"

"Is it a boy or a girl?" asked Jess, giggling.

"It's impossible to tell with a name like Dynamo," laughed Chloe.

"I must go and collect Pop and Lolly," Mrs. Lowther said to the person she was talking to. "They'll be waiting for me. Come on, girls," she added.

Backstage was chaos, with a confusion of models,

clothes and dressers, all packed together in a small space. Discarded clothes were being put on hangers and the models were trying to change back into their own clothes. Chloe was shocked. She had imagined that stars like Pop and Lolly would have dressing rooms of their own, but they were jumbled up with everyone else, with no privacy at all.

"It wouldn't do to be shy about getting changed if you were a model," Jess said quietly. Chloe agreed.

"Maybe that's why Mrs. Lowther didn't think it was odd to say we could be there while she was trying things on," she whispered. "If you're a model, it probably doesn't occur to you to be self-conscious."

"I wonder if she was a model when she was young?" said Jess.

Chloe glanced at the twins' mum, who was waving to attract Lolly's attention. "Maybe she was," she replied. "She's very glamorous."

Eventually, both Pop and Lolly were dressed and had fought their way out of the crush.

"Phew!" said Lolly. "Sorry to keep you waiting, but

it's bedlam in here. I lost my jeans, only to find that one of the other girls had put them on and was wondering why they didn't fit properly!"

"Are you sure you've got everything?" asked their mum.

Pop nodded. "All I want now is a drink," she said. "I'm parched."

"There's some water in the car," said Mrs. Lowther.

"Let's go then," said Lolly. "Did you enjoy the show?" she added, as they made their way to the lift.

"It was great!" said Jess.

As they waited for the lift, the twins were accosted by two girls about Chloe's age. "Can we have your autograph?" one of them asked Pop.

"Of course," said Pop graciously.

Both Pop and Lolly signed the Plumley's shopping bags that the girls offered them. Then they turned to Chloe and Jess. "Can we have yours too?" they asked.

Jess started to explain. "I'm not …" she started but Pop nudged her.

"Oh go on, Jessica," she urged in a loud voice.

"Don't be mean. The girls are really lucky to have met you as well." She winked and Chloe stifled a giggle. She and Jess added their names to the bags and then Mrs. Lowther guided her charges into the lift.

"They're going to spend ages trying to puzzle out who you are," said Pop to Jess with a smile.

"They have a couple of very rare bags now," said Lolly. "Signed by us all."

"But I'm not anyone," protested Jess.

"Of course you are," said Lolly. "Just because you're not famous it doesn't mean you're not someone special." Lolly beamed at her. "And from what I hear you might be in the Olympics one day. Then those girls will be glad they asked us all to sign their bags."

"I doubt it," said Jess, but she looked very pleased.

They soon got back to the car and all piled in.

"I can't wait to get home," said Pop impatiently. "Tara should be arriving soon, and then we can head off to the country!"

"Are we going tonight?" asked Chloe.

"Yes," said Lolly. "It'll only take a couple of hours if we can avoid the rush-hour traffic. Dad's coming too. He's been away on business, but he should be at the flat by now."

Sure enough, Mr. Lowther was there to greet them. He shook hands with Chloe and Jess and gave them a big smile. "Call me David," he said. "It's lovely to meet you both. I'm hoping you're going to help keep Pop under control while you're here." He gave the girls a wink, and Pop laughed.

"No chance!" she told him.

The girls went to pack their bags. When the doorbell rang Chloe looked at Jess. "Maybe that's Tara," she said. A few moments later the door opened and Tara came in, looking the happiest Chloe had seen her in a while. Chloe introduced her to Jess.

"Guess what?" Pop told Tara. "Jess is a hockey star!"

"No I'm not!" said Jess. But Tara wanted to hear all about it.

"I love hockey, but I'm hopeless at it," she told Jess. "I wish I had your talent."

Lolly met Chloe's eyes and smiled. Hopefully, Tara and Jess were going to get on well. Tara didn't give praise easily, so it was great she was impressed by Jess already.

"Come into the kitchen while I get another drink," said Lolly.

Chloe leaned against a cupboard while Lolly ran herself a glass of cool water. "Mum's been on at us for ages to have a clear out at home," Lolly told her. "If you're up for it we could do it while you're with us. I bet there's loads of stuff we could pass around... if you don't think Jess would be offended."

"I doubt it!" laughed Chloe. "Who *doesn't* like trying on clothes!"

"Tara!" said Lolly, laughing, as Pop, Jess and Tara appeared.

10 In the Country

Chloe was prepared for the Lowther's house to be big, but she and Jess were totally blown away when the car turned in at the open gate and pulled up outside. Jess clutched Chloe's arm. "It's *huge!*"

Despite its size, Chloe thought the house looked very welcoming in the early evening sun. It was built of soft, yellow stone, with large windows that looked out over a wide gravelled area and lawns beyond.

Mrs. Lowther stopped the car outside the wide front door and gave a contented sigh. "Home at last," she said.

Pop undid her seat belt, and leaned towards her mother. "Which rooms are Chloe, Jess and Tara having?" she asked.

In the Country

"Tara can have the yellow room," said Mrs. Lowther. "And I thought Chloe and Jess might like to share the nursery."

Chloe could feel Jess looking at her but she refused to meet her gaze. She didn't want anyone in the Lowther family to realize that she and Jess might not be overly enthusiastic about sleeping in a nursery! The yellow room sounded much more sophisticated.

They carried their bags into the large hall, which had dark, polished floorboards, and doors opening off in several directions. In front of them rose the stairs, and Pop eagerly led the way. "Come on!" she said. "If we hurry we can get you settled before it's time for dinner."

They saw Tara's room first. It was quite small, but beautifully furnished with antique furniture that gleamed with polish. And the mottled, butter-yellow wallpaper and duvet cover were lovely. Chloe and Jess exchanged glances and Chloe knew exactly what Jess was thinking. If only they could have a room like that!

But then, once Tara had dumped her bag, Lolly led them along a short corridor and threw open another door. Chloe gasped. One wall of the large room was taken up with a huge window. Below it was a comfy window seat, and the view, over the rear garden, was magnificent.

"Here you are," said Lolly, with a smile. "I hope you like it."

"It's a wonderful room!" said Chloe. She glanced at Jess and was rewarded with a beaming smile. Jess obviously liked it too.

The curtains and bedding glowed with bright Indian prints and weren't babyish at all. The only real evidence that it had once been a nursery was a large rocking horse with a rag doll perched on its saddle.

"Hello, Dobbin!" said Pop, hugging the spotted, wooden horse extravagantly and setting it rocking.

"And hello, Jemima," said Lolly quietly, catching the doll before it could slide to the floor.

"We keep talking about turning this into a proper guest suite, but Mum has never got round to it," said Lolly.

"It's perfect, just as it is," said Chloe. "And the view is fantastic!"

"And that's not all," said Pop, opening another door. "You have your own bathroom too."

The bathroom was wonderful, with two towelling bathrobes hanging up on the back of the door for them. Chloe felt as if she and Jess had just arrived at a very upmarket hotel. She wasn't at all envious of Tara now. After all, she'd have to pad along a corridor to get to her bathroom.

"Right," said Pop crisply, once they had seen the rooms. "Dinner will be in half an hour. I hope that's okay. I'm starving already."

"Me too!" said Chloe.

"We'll come and fetch you," added Lolly. "So don't worry about finding your way downstairs. We'll give you a proper guided tour after we've eaten. See you soon."

"Well!" said Jess as soon as the others had gone. She went and sat on the window seat, kicked her heels and grinned at Chloe. "This is fantastic!"

"Isn't it?" agreed Chloe. "Let's unpack. We are *so* going to enjoy our time here."

✳

Mrs. Lowther was on the phone when the girls eventually went down for their meal. "Honestly!" she said once she'd rung off. "I asked for a pink lining in the marquee, and now they say I can only have a white one."

"It won't matter," said Pop helpfully. "It means you can have lots of different-coloured flowers instead of just pink and white."

"The marquee is for Mum's party," Lolly explained to Chloe and Jess as they ate. "She has one every summer."

"And she gets totally stressed about all the tiniest details," said Pop with a grin.

Jess laughed, but stopped and looked embarrassed when Mrs. Lowther gave Pop a disapproving look.

"We mustn't forget to give you three a tour of the house," Lolly said, neatly changing the subject.

"Oh yes," Pop agreed at once. "We'll show you downstairs first, and end up in our bedrooms."

As soon as they'd finished eating together in the kitchen, Chloe, Jess and Tara followed the twins into the hall. Pop whisked them all over the house, chattering gaily as she went. After visiting the dining room with its huge polished table, the drawing room, their father's study, and the morning room, Pop led the way upstairs. They didn't bother with all the bedrooms. "They're all pretty similar really," she said dismissively. "But come and see the attic rooms."

At the top of the house it was like another world. Here, the ceilings sloped and the stairs were much narrower. But there were several rooms. "Years ago, houses like this had live-in servants," explained Lolly. "And they must have all lived up here."

The rooms were simply furnished, but looked comfortable enough to Chloe.

"Just think about the winters though," said Pop. "We've got central heating up here now, but it must have been freezing for them a hundred years ago. They wouldn't even have had warm water to wash in, unless they lugged it up the stairs!"

"Come on. We haven't got to our rooms yet," Lolly reminded Pop.

"Let's go there now," said Pop, closing the door of an attic room and heading for the stairs. "We kept the best for last!" She shot them a grin as she started down the narrow staircase.

"Wow!" Jess was seriously impressed by the Lowther twins' suite of rooms. Pop and Lolly had a big bedroom each, with connecting doors that led to a shared sitting room. It was a comfortable place, with easy chairs and a table large enough to do homework on or even to eat at. There was also a shared bathroom and next to that, another large room, fitted with floor-to-ceiling mirrored doors.

When Lolly opened the doors Jess gasped again. "And this is where we keep our clothes," Pop explained.

Lights came on inside, and the girls could see rails of clothes, with an aisle between them, and a large mirrored wall at the far end. There were also rows of pull-out baskets for tops, underclothes and shoes. The whole room was filled to bursting, and most of the baskets were a jumble of clothes, that spilled over onto the carpeted floor.

"It's a vast walk-in wardrobe," said Chloe admiringly. "It's bigger than my whole bedroom at home!"

"You can see why Mum wants us to have a clear-out," said Lolly ruefully. "It's our major task this holiday, now we've finished our modelling jobs."

Tara had been pretty quiet during the guided tour, but now she had something to say. "Well, if you plan on sorting clothes while I'm here, I'll go and do some songwriting," she said. "I brought my acoustic guitar, just in case I had some spare time."

The others laughed. "Trust you," teased Pop. "But why don't you serenade us while we sort?"

"I suppose I could do," said Tara.

"And we won't do *too* much clothes sorting while you're here, Tara. Promise!"

"Don't worry," grinned Tara. "I'll survive."

"Tell us about this summer party your mum is organizing," said Chloe once they were all comfortably settled in easy chairs. "It sounds really exciting."

"It would be if our friends were allowed to come," said Pop gloomily. "I asked if you could all stay for it but Mum wouldn't agree."

"It's a shame," said Tara. "Our mums know each other quite well," she explained to Jess and Chloe. "My parents get invited to the summer party every year. But I'll have to go and stay with my granny while they party. It would have made much more sense to stay here."

"Wouldn't it!" said Pop. "It's not fair. Mum expects us to be there, and she gets an amazing guest list of people coming, but none of them is anywhere near our age. And after a group of musicians let them down a few years ago she's insisted on hiring a terrible disco ever since."

"Well we think it's terrible," added Lolly. "But her friends seem to like it."

"It's a shame she won't use real musicians," said Tara.

"Why doesn't she use Rockley Park pupils as entertainers?" asked Jess.

Everyone stared at her, but no one said anything and she blushed. "Sorry!" she apologized. "What do I know? Of course it's a silly idea."

"No it's not," said Lolly. "Actually, it's not."

"I can't believe we haven't thought of it before," said Pop, her eyes shining.

"Hang on though. We did suggest we do a catwalk show a few years ago, and she hated the idea," said Lolly.

"But that *was* ages ago," protested Pop. "And it wasn't music. We're much older now. And think! We've got Chloe and Tara here already. If we got the boys along as well we'd have a great band."

"You mean have a Wizard Monkey Breath gig, here?" said Tara, looking astonished.

"Why not?" said Pop. "You could play *Sky Blue*."

"All Mum's friends would know the song that won the International Battle of the Bands," said Lolly thoughtfully. "I bet her guests would be really impressed."

The twins looked at their friends. "What do you

think? Would you like to play? It would mean staying on an extra couple of days."

Chloe and Tara stared at each other questioningly. "I don't see why not," said Tara slowly.

"But how long would we have to play for?" said Chloe. "After all, we don't have an hour's set rehearsed, or anything like!"

"But," Pop said, looking more and more excited "it wouldn't need to be just your band. We could all perform our end-of-term concert pieces. We can do those really professionally. And how about inviting Marmalade? He did a brilliant dance at the end-of-term concert. If he came too we could easily entertain the guests for an hour, or more, if they could stand it."

Pop and Lolly were grinning at each other. "It's the perfect way to get Mum to let us have our friends to the party!" laughed Pop.

Lolly turned to Jess. "How come you have such brilliant ideas?" she asked. "Three cheers for Jess!"

Chloe grinned at Jess. She felt really proud of her for fitting in so easily with the Rockley Park bunch. And to have come up with the idea of them performing at the summer party was brilliant.

Jess's face went as pink as her hair with pleasure. "And of course," she added happily, "you've got loads of spare rooms for people to stay in." Then she caught sight of the expression on Lolly's face and her smile faded. "What's the matter?" she asked. "What's up? Did I say something wrong?"

11 A Brilliant Idea

Lolly couldn't help looking sad. "It's just...there won't be any spare rooms," she said.

Pop butted in. "All the spare bedrooms are used for party guests," she explained. "We girls will be okay if you don't mind camping on our sitting-room floor, but what would we do with the boys?"

There was silence while everyone tried in vain to think of a solution.

"I don't suppose..." started Jess.

"What?" chorused the others.

"Well...it's what you said about us camping on the floor. Why can't we all, boys and girls, camp properly...

with tents and everything? There's loads of space outside."

Lolly's face lit up. "Camping is a great idea."

Tara was scowling, but then she often did that when she was thinking. "You mean like a back-to-front festival or something? All the performers in tents and the audience in proper beds? It's usually the other way round, you know."

"I know. It *would* be rather different," admitted Jess.

"But it would be fun," said Lolly, with a grin.

"Only if we're allowed to camp too," said Pop hurriedly. "It would be awful if we had to sleep indoors while everyone else was camping."

"My dad's got a tent," volunteered Tara. "He bought it a few years ago when he had the mad idea that Mum might enjoy camping." She shook her head. "I don't know what he was thinking of," she muttered, more to herself than anyone else.

"This is really exciting!" said Pop. "We could set up camp in the paddock next to the orchard. It's close enough for us to use the gardener's old outside loo.

I bet it still works, even though it's full of junk. We could take turns using our bathroom for showers. It'd be *sooo* cool!"

"Have you got a tent Chloe?" asked Lolly.

Chloe was still feeling astonished that any house would have a loo for the gardener, but she shook her head at Lolly's question. "'Fraid not," she said.

"I have!" volunteered Jess. Then her face fell. "But how would we get it here?" she asked.

Chloe had the answer to that. "Danny!" she said confidently. "He could bring it with him...oh! But what about his drum kit?" she added. "He'd never be able to cart it all this way on a bus, or a train!"

Lolly opened a drawer in the table and pulled out a large pad of paper. "We need to do some planning before we present this idea to our parents," she warned Pop. "We don't want Mum to say yes, and then find it's a non-starter."

"You're right!" agreed Pop. "At the very least we ought to make sure that the performers will be able to come. That means phoning up Danny, Ed, Ben and

Marmalade, but the mobile reception here is hopeless. We'll have to use the house phone."

"E-mail?"

"Good thinking, Jess," said Tara.

"We can share the jobs out," said Chloe.

"And while you're contacting people I'll be trying to think of other things we might need to do like...I don't know...getting hold of a sound system maybe?" said Jess.

Lolly pushed the pad and pen in Jess's direction. "Great!" she said. "Here you are. Put down anything you can think of that we might need."

Jess divided the page into two columns. "Performance," she wrote at the top of one column, and "Camping" at the other. Then she underlined both words. "Do either of you have a tent?" she asked Lolly, poised with her pen.

"There's an old, canvas one in the cellar," said Pop with a giggle. "I expect it was last used about a hundred years ago."

"But you asked for one a couple of Christmases

ago," said Lolly in a rush. "Don't you remember, Pop? It was all flowery, and you were going to camp out during the summer but you never did."

"Oh yes!" said Pop, leaping to her feet. "I wonder where it is?"

While Pop searched for her tent, Tara tapped the "Camping" column. "My tent sleeps two," she said.

"And mine does too," added Jess, writing busily.

A few minutes later, Pop appeared triumphantly with a long bag, made of bright pink and purple flowered fabric. It clanked slightly as she set it down on the carpet.

"Trust you to have a designer tent!" snorted Tara.

"We'd better try contacting people now, if that's okay with you," Pop said to Jess.

Jess waved a hand in reply, but didn't look up from her pad.

"Come on then, you lot," said Pop to Lolly, Chloe and Tara. "Let's leave Jess, the master list-maker, in peace. We need answers from the boys as soon as possible, so I think we ought to phone *and* e-mail.

A Brilliant Idea

One of us can use my laptop while I go downstairs to phone. See you in a few minutes, Jess."

It didn't take too long to get in touch with everyone. The band members jumped at the chance. Luckily, Ed and Ben weren't going away until after the party date, and Marmalade was delighted to be asked. Jess had done a tally of tents, and announced that if Danny and Ed brought theirs there would be plenty of space for all.

Chloe, Tara and the twins poured over Jess's lists. "You'll have to help me on the musical side," she told them. "I just put down what came to mind. I expect you'll have lots of other stuff to add on."

"Drums, sound system and stage," read Tara. "They are the things that really stand out now. Dad might be able to help with some advice, I suppose. He'll be back from Seattle tomorrow morning. I can ring him first thing."

"Hang on a minute," said Lolly. "Don't you think we ought to go and speak to *our* parents about it, Pop, before we start ringing other adults up, and getting them involved?"

"I can't see Mum turning down such a brilliant opportunity to entertain her guests," said Pop. "But we ought to tell her first, before we go any further. Let's go and see Mum and Dad now. They'll have finished watching the news, and they'll be in the drawing room together – in a mellow mood hopefully. It's the perfect time."

"D'you want us to come with you?" asked Chloe.

Lolly thought. "No, it's okay," she said. "If you, Jess and Tara come down, Mum might think we're trying to twist her arm. It's probably better if we keep it to a family discussion."

"Put the TV on if you're bored," said Pop, opening a cupboard and revealing a state-of-the-art entertainment system. "Or there's music, and loads of films to watch if you prefer. But I don't suppose we'll be long."

"It's so exciting," said Chloe. "I do hope they say yes."

"They'll be *thrilled*," said Pop confidently. "Mum always wants her summer party to be really successful, and this way it'll be the event of the season!"

A Brilliant Idea

Once Pop and Lolly had gone downstairs, Chloe put some music on. Jess and Tara soon got into a conversation about hockey. Chloe wasn't really interested, but she was pleased that Jess and Tara were getting on so well. She started looking through the twins' collection of films. There were loads of them, and quite a few she hadn't seen but liked the sound of. She was just wondering if it would be worth suggesting they put one on when Pop and Lolly came back, both looking rather upset.

"Well?" said Tara, seeing their faces. "Is it bad news?"

Pop plonked herself down beside Tara and folded her arms. "I can't *believe* it," she fumed.

Lolly sighed. "After all our careful planning," she said sadly.

"So," Chloe tried to find the right words, "they don't like the idea?"

Lolly looked awkward. "Dad seemed to think it would be all right," she said. "But…"

Pop butted in. "Basically, our mother thinks having a load of kids around at her precious party would ruin it," she told them. "She seems to think we'd all behave like two-year-olds, or trash the place. She is *soo* out of touch."

Tara shrugged. "Well there's nothing you can do about it," she said.

"That's right," agreed Chloe. "It was a neat idea. But it's her party."

"I don't care," said Pop hotly. "I feel like phoning all her friends and getting them to demand that we perform!"

"Oh, Pop," said Lolly. "You always overreact. Don't make things worse, she'll only accuse us of tricking her into it."

"Well she makes me so mad!" huffed Pop. "We offer all this free entertainment and she acts as if we want to throw ice cream at her guests."

"Never mind," said Chloe, struggling to be positive. "We can still have a lovely time over the next couple of days."

"Come on," said Lolly. "Let's think about something else. I'm really sorry it didn't work out, but we mustn't waste the rest of your time here."

"How about watching a film?" suggested Chloe, trying to help Lolly lift the atmosphere. "You've got loads of good ones."

After a few minutes' discussion they chose a film and soon everyone was absorbed in the action. As soon as it was over, Chloe and Jess got up to go to their room, but Lolly stopped them.

"Don't go yet," she begged. "It's our first night together, and Pop and I have finished work for the summer. We mustn't let anything get in the way of having fun. Let's have a midnight feast."

Pop stared at her sister. "Well Miss Goody-Goody!" she teased. "I never thought I'd hear that suggestion coming from you. Excellent idea!"

Trying not to make any noise, the girls crept downstairs to the kitchen. The pantry floor was tiled, and very chilly on their bare feet.

"Hurry up!" begged Jess, hopping from one foot to the other. "Why didn't I bring my slippers?"

"Ssh," said Pop, handing her a huge bag of crisps.

Lolly handed Chloe a cake tin and added a bottle of cola to her own stash.

"Can we have these?" asked Tara, holding up a bunch of bananas.

"If you want," said Pop with a giggle.

They made their way back upstairs and along the corridor. With each creaking floorboard they had to stifle their laughter, and when Jess's crisp packet slid from her grasp and fell with a crackle to the floor, they just about doubled up. At last they made it back to Pop and Lolly's sitting room and flung themselves onto the squashy sofas.

"Are we downhearted?" asked Pop, through a mouthful of chocolate brownie.

"No!" replied Chloe, taking her second from the tin.

"We'll find a way to change Mum's mind," said Lolly with determination.

"Bound to," agreed Tara. "Especially with Jess here."

Chloe and Jess exchanged happy smiles. They might be disappointed about the concert, but they were still having *such* a cool time.

12 An Outrageous Plan

The next day, the girls decided to spend some time sorting out the twins' clothes. Even Tara got drawn into the fun. She would have run a mile rather than try anything on, but she sprawled on a sofa and made silly comments at everything the others tried.

Soon there were a couple of heaps of clothes on the floor, mostly destined for charity or recycling.

"I can't believe you've still got that old swimsuit!" yelped Pop as Lolly pulled a faded pink one out of a drawer.

"Well," said Lolly, looking at it fondly, "don't you remember that holiday in Jamaica? We had such a good time."

"But we were *six* then!" said Pop. "It can't have fitted you for years."

"Recycling," proclaimed Tara. "You can't charity-shop it. It's lost its elastic. Imagine some poor child jumping into a swimming pool in it. It would fall off as soon as it got wet!" Chloe and Jess laughed.

"You're right," said Pop. "It can go to be shredded and made into something else." She tossed it onto the recycling heap, ignoring Lolly's rather regretful expression.

By the time the twins had gone through half their wardrobe, Chloe and Jess were proud owners of some stunning cast-offs, and it was lunchtime. "Let's go and eat," suggested Lolly. "I'm starving."

They all trooped downstairs. As they went through the hall the house phone rang and Pop picked it up.

"Oh hi!" she said after a couple of seconds. She listened carefully while the others waited for her. "I'm not sure," she said at last. "But I'll find out." She shot a glance in Tara's direction and winked. "Actually, there's someone here you know," she said. "It's Tara, the bassist and songwriter from Wizard Monkey Breath. In fact Chloe is here too. Would you like a word with them while I go and ask Mum? Okay. Hang on."

Tara was looking bewildered and grumpier by the moment, but Pop put her hand over the phone and explained. "It's Sebastian Walters," she said in a loud whisper.

Jess gasped and stared at Chloe. Sebastian Walters was the mega-famous TV chat show host, who had introduced Tara's band at a huge charity gig, shortly after they'd won the International Battle of the Bands in Italy. He'd chatted to all the band members, including vocalist Chloe, and had given Tara a lovely replacement for her songwriting notebook, which she had tragically lost. He obviously remembered her, because Pop said "Here she is," and handed the phone straight to Tara.

While Tara was speaking to Sebastian Walters, Pop pulled the rest of the girls into a huddle. "I'm going to ask him if he'll try to get Mum to change her mind," she whispered. "I'm sure he will."

"You can't do that!" Lolly whispered back, looking scandalized.

"Just watch me," replied Pop.

"You said you were going to fetch Mum," Lolly reminded her, in an appalled voice.

Pop tried to look wide-eyed and innocent. "I can't find her at the moment," she said.

Lolly groaned. "You're *dreadful*," she complained. "If Mum finds out you've been trying to manipulate her guests she'll go *ballistic*."

Tara was saying goodbye. She covered the phone with her hand and beckoned to Chloe. "He wants to say hello to you too," she said.

As Chloe took the phone she was aware of a furious, whispered argument continuing in the hall. There was no way Lolly was going to agree to Pop's proposal, but Chloe wasn't sure Lolly had much of an option.

"So what are you up to this summer?" Sebastian Walters asked Chloe.

"Not a lot really," she told him, trying to concentrate

on his words. "Here for a few days with Pop and Lolly and then back at home with my little brother."

"I was telling Tara," he said. "It's a shame you have to go home before the party. It would have been nice to see you again."

"Yes," agreed Chloe, feeling awkward. "It would have been good."

Just then Pop grabbed her arm and pointed to the phone.

"Oh! Here's Pop again," Chloe told him. "I'd better hand you over."

"Take care then," said Sebastian Walters. "I hope we meet again soon."

"Me too," agreed Chloe.

Pop took the phone, looking very determined. "I've got a favour to ask," she said straight away. "No," she admitted after listening to him. "I haven't even gone to look for her. I'll get her to ring you back. But wait. This is important."

Everyone was listening to Pop.

"Please ask Mum if we can all perform for her

guests," Pop was begging Sebastian. "We'd be much better than a stupid disco, but she just can't see it. I'm sure if you suggested us she'd realize what a brilliant idea it was."

Lolly had her head in her hands, but Tara was looking amused, and Jess was obviously excited to be in on the whole thing. Chloe went up to Lolly and gave her a quick hug.

"It's not your fault," she whispered. "If it all comes out and your mum is angry I'm sure she'll realize it was Pop, not you who asked him. She must know what she's like."

Lolly gave Chloe a lopsided smile. "Of course she does," she said. "But I always feel as if I ought to be able to talk her out of her most outrageous schemes. The thing is," she added, "I don't blame her for having the cheek to try, even though he'll never do as she's asked. The summer party is usually so boring for us."

Pop put the phone down and gave everyone a cheeky grin. "Phew!" she said. "I suppose I'd better go and tell Mum that Sebastian Walters phoned, and that he'd like her to call him back."

She disappeared down the hall with her fingers firmly crossed behind her back.

"Well," said Lolly in response to all the quizzical looks she was getting, "I don't know what he said, any more than you do." She looked rather nervous. "No doubt Pop will tell us eventually. Shall we go and find some lunch?"

Mrs. Lowther was in the kitchen, but Pop wasn't there, so Lolly gave her mother the message. "Pop spoke to him," she said hurriedly when Mrs. Lowther asked what the call had been about. "I think she went into the garden to find you."

"Silly girl," said Mrs. Lowther. "She should have known I would be making lunch."

"I expect she'll find us," said Lolly, taking salad out of the enormous fridge.

"Can we help?" asked Chloe.

By the time Pop appeared, Chloe and Jess had set out plates and cutlery on the large kitchen table, while

Tara had made a jug of squash. Pop gave her mother the message too, with a straight face. "He said this afternoon would do," she added and joined the others, helping herself to salad and fresh, crusty bread.

"Anyone fancy taking a rug out to the garden this afternoon?" Pop piped up. "It's a gorgeous day for a swim."

Everyone liked that idea, but Chloe remembered the heaps of clothes they'd abandoned in the twins' room.

"Don't worry," said Pop, gaily chasing the problem away with a wave of her hand. "We can finish that this evening. It's much too nice to be indoors this afternoon."

"You're right, darling," said Mrs. Lowther. "And I'm so pleased you've made a start on your clothes. I expect I have your visitors to thank for that. Pop and Lolly would never have got going without you to spur them on." She smiled at Chloe, and Chloe smiled back. "I hope you, Tara and Jess have found a few things you can use," she added, taking in Tara's black T-shirt and shorts. "My girls have far too many clothes, and you all need *something* to repay you for your hard work."

"Come on then," said Pop, without giving Chloe an opportunity to reply. "Let's go!"

In no time they were all outdoors, heading for the pool. It was surrounded by a sheltering wall, and had a small, wooden chalet changing room. There was a fridge stocked with drinks, sunloungers nearby, and a couple of large umbrellas for shade.

"This is so cool!" said Jess, taking in the whole scene. "And look at these," she added, picking up a basket of inflatable toys. "Can we try blowing some of them up? They'd be such a laugh in the water."

"Of course," laughed Lolly, pulling a plastic shape out of the basket. I think this is an inflatable chair. We had a great time with it in the pool last summer."

Lolly started looking for the air pump, but Pop caught her arm to stop her. "Don't you want to know what Sebastian said?"

"I expect he told you what a cheek you have!" she said.

"Go on then, what *did* he say?" asked Tara.

They all sat on the edge of the pool, with their legs dangling in the cool water while Pop talked.

"I told him what our plans had been," she said excitedly. "And he said that when he spoke to Mum later he'd sort of make it obvious to her that he assumed we'd be performing at the party, because we've been at Rockley Park for a while, and have such famous friends!"

"You are beyond belief!" said Lolly, trying to look stern and failing.

"That's brilliant!" said Chloe. "I would never have had the guts to ask a thing like that. I'd have been too scared that my parents would find out and go crackers!"

"Me too," agreed Jess admiringly. "You do have a nerve. But how come your mother knows people like Sebastian Walters?"

Pop shrugged. "Oh well, you know..." she said. "Mum used to be a model before she had us, so she knows people in the fashion industry. And these days she gets involved with all sorts of charity functions.

Poor Dad isn't particularly interested in celebrities. He's an industrialist, but he's very supportive of Mum."

Lolly smiled. "She's a whizz at getting celebrities to contribute! She can twist them round her little finger."

Tara snorted. "So that's where Pop gets it from," she said. "And thanks to her cheek we're on!"

"Hopefully," said Pop with a giggle. "Give it time. I reckon we'll get the go-ahead very soon."

Even Lolly was looking excited now. "I think Sebastian Walters must be as bad as you, Pop," said Lolly. "He can't have needed too much encouragement."

"That's true!" said Pop. "He thought it was a great laugh that I was asking. But he did say he thought it was a seriously good idea as well," she added.

"He's not stupid," put in Tara. "I'm sure if he thought it would backfire he wouldn't say a word. And he was so kind to me when I lost my notebook. He's a really nice person."

"Well, I'm sorry I tried to talk you out of it," Lolly said to Pop. "But I don't have your nerve."

"Don't worry about it," said Pop, giving her sister a shove, so that she landed in the water with a squeal and a big splash. "I forgive you," she added, jumping in too, along with the others. "And if it all goes wrong I'll own up straight away."

"I know you will," said Lolly, ducking her twin sister under the water. "Because if you don't I'll kill you!"

Chloe thought they might hear something when they went back indoors at the end of the afternoon, but although they saw Mrs. Lowther briefly, she didn't mention Sebastian Walters or the party. Pop wanted to ask, but Lolly managed to persuade her to wait.

"If she goes for it we'll hear soon enough," she said wisely. "But if you pester her you might put her off. You know how much she hates being pushed into anything."

"You're right," agreed Pop. "But waiting is so hard!"

It wasn't until much later that evening, after dinner, when Mr. and Mrs. Lowther asked their daughters to join them in the drawing room. "I hope you'll excuse us," David Lowther said to Chloe, Jess and Tara. "But the twins won't be long."

"That's okay," said Chloe hastily. "We'll be fine."

The three friends went up to the old nursery to wait.

"I hope it'll be all right," said Chloe. "Lolly looked really worried."

About an hour after the twins had gone to speak to their parents they burst into the nursery.

"We wondered where you'd gone when we couldn't find you in our sitting room," said Lolly.

"We found some board games in the nursery cupboard," explained Chloe. "I hope that's okay. But actually we've been too anxious to concentrate."

"Well?" demanded Jess, unable to wait a moment longer. "What happened?"

"She said yes!" Pop burst out.

"We've been so long because we were discussing how to make it work at such short notice," added Lolly. "Dad is going to ring the marquee company first thing in the morning to see if they can provide a stage and sound system to add on to the end of the marquee, and we've got to come up with a programme of acts so Mum knows how much time to allow for it all."

"She thought camping was a brilliant idea," laughed Pop. "Sorry, Jess, Sebastian Walters presented everything, as his idea of course, so you won't get any acknowledgment from the adults, but I think it was the camping that finally swung it. If Mum had needed to put everyone up she would have had to say no."

"Jess will be able to stay for the party, won't she?" put in Tara.

"Of course she will." Lolly looked shocked at the thought that she might not. "We told Mum that Jess is an essential part of our team, which is true! You can't miss out on the fun, Jess, after coming up with the most superb ideas anyone has had so far this holiday!"

Jess turned to Chloe with shining eyes. "This is amazing!" she said. "I'd never have dreamed that this summer holiday would turn out to be so fantastic!"

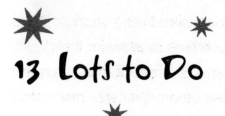

13 Lots to Do

The following day the girls had to get organized. There was so much to do it was scary. Mrs. Lowther's summer party was only a few days away, and the biggest worry for Chloe had been that she and Jess might not be allowed to stay for longer, but when she phoned, her mum didn't have any objections. "I'm glad you're having such a good time," she said. "And I'll tell Jess's mum what's happening. She's coming home tonight. Can I give her Mrs. Lowther's number, so she can phone if she wants to?"

"Jess has already texted her mum," said Chloe. "And she said it was okay."

"Well, all right," said Chloe's mum. "But I'll give

her a ring as well, just to be sure."

As soon as that was settled, Jess was unanimously voted the coordinator, and, she decided that the first thing to do was to put the programme together.

"You ought to open the show," Jess said to the twins. "As you're part of the host family."

"Okay," agreed Lolly.

"And I bet Sebastian Walters would agree that Wizard Monkey Breath ought to be the finale," said Pop.

"Okay," said Jess, noting it down. "Chloe, are you going to be doing a solo as well as singing with the band?"

"Yes, do!" urged Lolly.

"Okay," agreed Chloe, looking pleased at the suggestion.

By the time they added in Marmalade's dance and the possibility of Tara playing her new song with her father, Jess's scribbled programme was looking quite varied and very good. If everyone performed two songs there would be plenty to entertain Mrs. Lowther's guests.

"Let's go and see how Dad is getting on with organizing the stage and sound system," said Pop. "Hopefully he'll have heard back by now. And he said he was going to ask the farmer next door if he'd cut the paddock for us. At the moment the grass is a bit long for camping."

They all went to Mr. Lowther's study and knocked on the door. Pop didn't wait for an answer, but walked right in. "What's the matter?" she asked straight away.

Chloe could see that Pop's father didn't look very happy. For a moment she wondered if it was because they were all invading his privacy, but he actually looked quite pleased to see them.

"It's the marquee people," he told them. "They say they can supply an extension to the tent, and staging for you in it, but a sound system is out of the question. I've just phoned the DJ your mother booked, but he says his system isn't suitable for you to use either."

"What about other companies that hire out sound systems?" Lolly suggested. "There must be quite a few around, surely?"

Summer Spectacular

Mr. Lowther shook his head. "Not many," he told her. "And I've tried them. I even tried a couple in London, but they all say the same thing. It's the summer. There are parties and festivals everywhere at the moment and they are fully booked. If we wanted to be sure of the equipment we needed we should have booked it months ago. I don't know what your mother will say," he added.

"I do," said Pop. "She'll say we ought to forget the idea, and that it was stupid to even consider it. But we can't let anything stop us now! We've got to find a way."

Mr. Lowther smiled at his daughter. "You're like a dog with a bone," he told Pop.

"Could you do an acoustic set?" asked Jess wistfully. Chloe could see that her friend was desperate for the performances to take place.

But Tara shook her head. "Chloe's the only one with a powerful enough voice to perform without a microphone," she explained. "I could play my acoustic bass with my dad on saxophone, but we'd still need something to boost the sound. It's just too big a gathering to have no amplification at all."

"And as soon as you use microphones you need a mixing desk, to get the levels right, so no one instrument drowns out another," explained Chloe.

"We could ask the DJ to play our backing tracks," said Lolly. "But with no microphones, you would hardly hear us singing along to them."

"He'll have a microphone to introduce the songs he plays at the disco," said Pop. "But it'll almost certainly be mounted near his decks, not on a stand, which is what we'd need. And no way would he have drum mics, or amps for the guitars, or even more than one microphone in total. Wizard Monkey Breath uses *loads* of equipment."

"To be fair, we do have our own amps," said Tara. "If we can manage to get them here. But none of us has a mixing desk, or the means to hook up to one. And I'm certain that Danny doesn't own a set of drum mics."

"Well that's that then," said Jess, looking and sounding really sad.

"No way!" protested Pop. "We just have to come up with *something*."

"If we don't get it sorted out, I'm going to need to tell your mum this afternoon," Mr. Lowther warned his daughter. "We can't mislead her. It wouldn't be fair."

"I'll phone Judge Jim," said Tara. "He'll know what to do."

Judge Jim Henson was head of the Rock Department at Rockley Park School, and was also a close friend of Tara's father. Because Tara's parents were so often away he was like a stand-in parent for her, and he was invariably the person she turned to in a crisis.

"Good call!" said Lolly approvingly. "I expect we can borrow the equipment from school."

"Go on then," urged Pop. "Do it now, Tara!"

Mr. Lowther offered Tara the phone on his desk. "Shall we leave you to it?" he asked Tara.

"No. It's okay," said Tara. "It'll only take a few minutes."

All eyes were on Tara as she dialled the number.

The phone rang for a while, and Tara was returning the handset to its cradle when Judge Jim finally answered.

"Hi!" said Tara. "Yes, fine. You?"

They waited while Tara and Judge Jim chatted. Chloe tried to work out how the conversation was going, but it was impossible. At last Tara said her goodbyes and rang off.

"Well?" demanded Pop. "What did he say?" Everyone, including Mr. Lowther, was waiting anxiously for her response.

Tara smiled. "Well, he *can* help."

The girls all gave a cheer, and Mr. Lowther looked pleased.

"We can't borrow any of the school equipment because it's needed for the summer schools they have over the holidays," said Tara. "But...Judge Jim has a mixing desk of his own that we could borrow, and some other bits and pieces too, microphones and cables and stuff. He said that if we can use the DJ's speakers as well it would be a help." She turned to Mr. Lowther. "Do you think he'd let us do that?"

David Lowther shrugged. "I could phone him back and ask him," he said. "But will it be reliable, having bits cobbled together from several sources?"

"If Judge Jim reckons it'll be all right, I'm sure it will," said Tara confidently. "He's a professional. There's no way he'd compromise a performance with dodgy equipment."

"All right then. I'll do it." Mr. Lowther tried the DJ's number, but it was engaged. "I'll try again later," he assured them. "And I'll let you know as soon as I do. Fingers crossed it'll be all right."

The girls left him to it and went out into the garden to enjoy the sun. By the time they went back indoors it was lunchtime. Chloe wanted to ask Mr. Lowther if he'd managed to contact the DJ, but she didn't feel she could while Mrs. Lowther was there as well. But while his wife was getting something out of the fridge he gave them all a wink and thumbs up. Pop grinned, and Chloe breathed a sigh of relief. It was going to be all right.

14 Campsite

That afternoon they cleaned out the old gardener's loo, for the campers to use. It was full of old spiderwebs and blown-in leaves. Chloe didn't mind most spiders, but there were a couple of huge black ones that she wasn't too keen on. Tara had no patience with squeamishness, and she swiftly sent them scurrying with her broom.

"They'll probably run straight back in when we're not looking," warned Pop, polishing the old, spotted mirror that hung above the washbasin.

"Well I'll try really hard not to need the loo in the night then," said Jess with a shudder.

Summer Spectacular

The following day lots happened. The marquee people arrived with a large lorry packed full of equipment, and the performers started to arrive as well. Danny was the first to turn up. His mum had put him on an early train, and Mr. Lowther volunteered to collect him from the station.

"Anyone want to come for the ride?" he asked.

Jess wanted to stay with Pop to watch the marquee go up, and Lolly was helping her mum with final meal planning for the many guests who would be staying for the party weekend. Tara had been inspired to write, and was in the garden, making up song lyrics, so Chloe volunteered to go. She liked Mr. Lowther more and more as she got to know him. He was kind, and funny, and showed a genuine interest in Chloe. On the way to the station she told him all about herself and her family, and about Danny and his phenomenal drumming ability.

"I'm looking forward to having a few boys around the place," he told her. "I'm rather outnumbered in this family."

It was clear to Chloe that although he loved his family dearly, he tended not to involve himself too much in what went on. Chloe got the impression that he found it easier that way.

Danny got off the train with two rolled-up tents and a rucksack. He looked rather anxious. Chloe hurried to greet him.

"Oh you're here," he said thankfully. "I was afraid I wouldn't be able to find the person who was supposed to be collecting me."

"You needn't have worried," laughed Chloe, taking one of the tents from him. "You're the only person here who looks as if they might be going camping. I'm so glad you've come," she added as they made their way towards Mr. Lowther. "This party is going to be so much fun, and camping will be brilliant too."

"I brought Jess's tent," said Danny. "Her mum's back from holiday. She said she had a lovely time."

"Good," said Chloe, who was pleased things had turned out so well for Jess and her mum.

Mr. Lowther put Danny's luggage in the boot and

then shook his hand. "Thank goodness!" he told him with a smile. "Another man. I've been outnumbered by all these girls for far too long."

"We're not that bad, are we?" teased Chloe as they all got into the car.

"No," he agreed. "You're not. And Pop and Lolly are having so much fun with you here. I'm really glad Leela decided to ask you to perform. Leela is my wife," he added for Danny's benefit. "And the twins' mother."

"Have the drums been sorted out okay?" asked Danny. "Chloe told me you were hiring some."

"Yes," said Mr. Lowther. "I managed to get hold of some for you, so I hope they'll be all right."

"That's good," said Danny, looking relieved. "They are almost sure to be better than mine, so thanks very much."

By the time they got back from the station, the garden was a hive of activity. The main marquee was already up, and the floor was being laid. The farmer had been in to cut the paddock, and Ed and

Ben had arrived in Ed's dad's car, with their amps and guitars.

They went out to the paddock. Pop and Lolly had dug their dad's ancient tent out and were laying poles and brown canvas out on the grass.

"I don't know how to put it up," said Pop, "and it doesn't seem to have a groundsheet, but it's going to be really big."

"It's an old army tent," said David Lowther. "I'd forgotten we even had it. You can't possibly sleep in that. The canvas is probably rotten."

"But we thought we could use it as a sort of sitting area, in case it rains," said Pop.

"And we have Pop's flowery tent to actually sleep in," added Lolly.

Once the tents were up, and instruments stowed safely indoors, everyone went for a swim. It was fun having Ed, Ben and Danny there, and it would be even better once Marmalade arrived.

"Inflatables!" yelled Ben, grabbing the pump. The boys blew them all up, and found that only a couple had punctures. Soon the pool was filled with a floating selection of animals, balls and a couple of blow-up chairs.

"That chair won't hold both of you," said Chloe, as Danny and Ben fought for possession of it. There was a lot of splashing, and a lot of noise, and after a while, they threw all the toys, except the ball, onto the side of the pool, to make some space in the water. They had a couple of races, and then climbed out to dry off in the sun.

"Phew!" said Jess after narrowly beating Danny. "I'm exhausted!"

"And I'm starving," said Pop.

Mrs. Lowther had ordered pizzas from the caterers who were doing the food for her party, and as soon as they were delivered everyone took slices and ate them on the lawn. After lunch, Mr. Lowther came over to the camp, and showed everyone how to make a fire pit, so they could safely boil a kettle and cook.

"You don't need to have a fire, or cook on it if you don't want to," he said. "But in my opinion this is at least half the fun. I can get a load of wood delivered if you want. And I'm sure there are some cooking pots to go with the old tent. You could make porridge for breakfast!"

Pop wrinkled her nose, but Tara looked enthusiastic. "With blueberries, or dried fruit," she said. "It'll be delicious."

Mr. Lowther smiled at her approvingly. "That's the spirit!" he said. "I can see you're a born backwoods-woman!"

Chloe had never had the opportunity to cook on an open fire. "Mightn't it be dangerous?" she asked.

"Yes, if you had the fire pit too close to the tents," agreed Mr. Lowther. "But this is a sensible distance away. Of course it's a good idea to keep some water nearby, just in case, and we'll cover the pit last thing at night in case of stray sparks. That'll make the fire safe, but the embers should keep glowing overnight, so all you'll have to do in the morning is feed them with a few twigs and you should soon get the fire blazing again."

Chloe was very impressed. "How did you learn all this?" she asked.

"My younger brother and I used to run wild in the summer holidays," he said. "We were country children, and got up to all sorts of mischief. It's amazing we didn't kill ourselves with some of our escapades. But along the way we learned all about campfires." He sighed. "It was a great childhood, but I haven't been camping for years. My wife was brought up in India. She'd never been camping as a child, and didn't like the idea. Pop and Lolly were never very interested in that sort of thing either."

"Well we are now!" said Lolly, giving her father a hug.

Mrs. Lowther wasn't very keen on keeping the fire alight over night. She thought it was far too dangerous unless there was an adult to keep an eye on the children. "And I've no idea who would be prepared to do that," she fussed. It was last thing at night, and while they were all in the kitchen, washing up the mugs they'd used to make themselves hot chocolate.

Lolly and Chloe exchanged looks. No one had thought about having an adult to camp with them.

"Don't worry," Mr. Lowther told his wife. "I will."

"You?" She looked astonished.

"Yes." He looked rather embarrassed. "I came across my little two-man tent when I went to find the cooking pots. It's in much better condition than that old army tent the girls found. You don't mind, do you?" he asked his daughters and their friends. "Only it is important to have an adult on hand. Don't worry. I won't pitch too close to you. And I won't interfere."

"That's fine by me!" said Danny. "It's really good of you to let us camp in the first place." Ed and Ben nodded in agreement.

"Maybe you'll be able to show us how to cook that porridge in the morning," added Tara with a grin.

In the gathering dusk, Mr. Lowther quickly pitched his tent. Then he put some squares of turf over the dying embers of the fire and drizzled water over the turf. "I'll be out later on to sleep," he told them. "Enjoy the rest of the evening."

Summer Spectacular

For a while the friends sat around by the tents chatting. There were some straw bales for them to sit on, so they were pretty comfortable. But once it had been properly dark for a while a chilly breeze began to blow. The big old army tent wasn't much better, because it let in so many draughts. "Brr...I'm going to get into my sleeping bag," said Pop.

"Me too," said Chloe.

Soon they were all in their tents. Chloe could hear the boys still talking nearby in the quiet night. The girls' tents were facing each other so they could chat from their sleeping bags with the tent flaps open. Jess and Chloe were together in Jess's tent, while the twins and Tara were squeezed into Pop's flowery one until Tara's dad brought hers.

"You look very squashed in there," observed Jess. "Are you all right?"

"Just about," said Pop, wriggling a bit. "Like sardines!"

"Loads is happening tomorrow!" said Jess excitedly. "I can't believe I'm going to meet the famous Judge

Jim Henson. Remember when we found him in our local record shop, Chloe, on a CD with loads of other famous musicians? That was during the first half term after you'd gone to Rockley Park. I was so impressed you knew him."

"And the day after tomorrow it's the party!" said Pop. "Thanks to you, Jess, I'm looking forward to Mum's summer party for the first time in my life!"

"It'll be fun," said Lolly with a yawn.

The girls kept talking for ages, but eventually they were all having trouble staying awake.

"I can't keep my eyes open any longer," said Lolly at last. "Anyway, it's too dark to see!"

"Fair enough," said Tara, pulling the tent flaps together and zipping them up. "Night all."

Jess and Chloe zipped up their tent too and snuggled down in the dark. "Night!" called Chloe.

"Night," answered Pop.

The boys called their goodnights, and Chloe could hear them zip up their tents. In spite of being so tired, Chloe was sure she'd never be able to sleep. The lilo from the pool that she was lying on wasn't anything like as comfortable as her mattress at home. Every time she moved it squeaked, and made her want to giggle. And she could hear every possible night-time noise through the thin tent wall. She and Jess talked quietly for a while, but eventually they started to doze, and by the time Mr. Lowther came to check on them, everybody was fast asleep.

15 Silence

It was very early when Chloe woke, but even so, someone was up before her. When she poked her head out of the tent she saw Tara, busy doing something by the fire pit. Chloe scrambled out of her sleeping bag, being careful not to disturb Jess, who was still fast asleep.

"Look!" said Tara in a low voice, when Chloe joined her. "The fire *is* still alight."

Tara had pulled the charred turf away and found the embers still glowing.

"Let's see if we can get it going properly," suggested Chloe.

Together they carefully fed the embers some tiny

bits of dry bark and twigs. Tara blew gently and soon a trickle of smoke appeared. "Just like Mr. Lowther said!" grinned Tara, once the twigs had burst into flame. They started feeding the fire with larger bits of wood. "He put just enough water on to stop the turf being totally burned and not enough to put the fire out. Clever!"

Chloe filled the kettle and put it on the fire. By the time the others started emerging from their tents into the early morning sunshine, it was almost boiling.

"Cool!" said a tousled Danny when he joined them. "Is there enough water for tea?"

Chloe didn't usually drink tea, but this smoky cup tasted delicious, made with the water she and Tara had boiled on the campfire.

"Are we going to have the sound system going today so we can rehearse?" asked Ed when he and Ben got up.

"I should think so," said Tara. "Judge Jim and my dad are coming to set it up. I hope Dad doesn't forget to bring my Rickenbacker. I did ask him to."

"Give him another ring," said Ben. "Just in case."

"Judge Jim will soon get us set up," said Ed. "It's not long since the end of term concert, so we don't need to have loads of rehearsals, but it'll be good to have a quick run-through."

"Marmalade should be here by lunchtime," said Danny. "I'm looking forward to seeing him again."

"Me too," said Chloe. "Rehearsals this afternoon then, and the party tomorrow. Bliss!"

Soon, Mr. Lowther poked his head out of his tent. It made Chloe laugh to see him looking as dishevelled as everyone else, when usually he was so elegant.

"Good gracious!" he said when he saw the crackling fire and singing kettle. "The fire stayed in. How did that happen?" But he didn't look at all surprised. He sent Pop and Lolly off to fetch bacon and rolls from the kitchen. Soon the aroma of frying was hanging in the air. "Not for me thanks," he said when Tara offered him a bacon roll. Then he hesitated. "Oh all right then," he said with a grin. "I can't resist. But I'd better eat it as I go. I'm off to shower and change. Lots to do. See you later."

Summer Spectacular

It was still quite early by the time everyone had eaten. But once they had all showered and cleared away the breakfast things, the sun was high in the sky and it was getting hot. They went over to the front of the house, where the marquee was pitched. Already, several workmen were there, putting the finishing touches to the stage and carting in tables and chairs for the meal that would precede the entertainment. In the hall were cases of wine, boxes of plates and glasses, heaps of pink tablecloths, and baskets full of cutlery.

"Should we offer to help set all the tables?" wondered Chloe.

"No. Don't worry," Lolly told her. "The caterers do it. Today is all about getting the furniture in position. In the morning a whole army of different people will arrive. They'll set the tables and stay on to waitress in the evening. You'll see."

"Some of them will be gap-year students, I expect," said Pop. "They're really friendly. It looks like hard work, but great fun too. They get to meet loads of interesting people, and see some wonderful entertainment." She gave a laugh. "Well, they're *bound* to see some amazing entertainers here!"

At midday, Marmalade arrived. "Thanks so much for including me," he said to Pop and Lolly. "It's sooo great to be with you guys again. I was missing you all." He threw his arms wide to include them all, and caught sight of Jess. "Wow!" he said, shaking his long, ginger curls. "Introduce me! At last, hair to rival mine!"

"He's always this daft," Chloe told Jess apologetically. "Don't take any notice."

Marmalade came over and grabbed Jess's hand. "Pleased to meet you," he told her, pumping her hand up and down in a ridiculous manner. "You have to admit," he told everyone with a grin, "ginger and pink make a lovely couple!" He put his head next to Jess's and fluttered his eyelashes.

Jess burst out laughing and pushed him away. "I've heard all about *you*," she teased.

While they waited for the sound system to arrive, the boys started to play an impromptu game of football.

"We want to play too!" yelled Pop as Marmalade dribbled the ball past her tent.

"Well put some shoes on then," said Ben. "You can't be on my team if you're wearing flip-flops!"

"Jess, come and join our team," called Danny, who knew about her prowess on the hockey pitch.

Chloe and Lolly looked at each other. "Do you want to play?" asked Lolly.

"As long as we don't take it too seriously," said Chloe. "I'm hopeless at ball games!"

"Okay then," said Lolly. "Let's join Marmalade's team. He never takes *anything* very seriously!"

The two friends had just done up their shoes when something caught Chloe's eye. "It's Judge Jim!" she said. "Hey, you lot! Judge Jim has arrived."

At once the football was abandoned, and the popular teacher was surrounded.

"Have you brought all the equipment?" Ben asked, once everyone had said their hellos.

Judge Jim nodded. "But it's goin' to need patchin' up a bit," he told them. "It's all bits an' pieces. But with your dad's help, Tara, it should be okay. It's just a matter of connectin' everythin' up right."

"Well we've got loads of time," said Chloe cheerfully.

"Did Dad come with you?" asked Tara. "He said he would. And did he remember my Rickenbacker?"

"Yep," said Judge Jim, nodding his head so his long, grey dreadlocks shook. "He's with the Lowthers at the moment. I said I'd come and find you lot because it'll be good to have help to unload. I see you've got a pretty fine camp here," he added. "Good job I don' have to camp. My old bones wouldn' stand it."

Judge Jim had never quite recovered since breaking a leg just over a year ago, and now he used a stick. Chloe could quite see that he wouldn't want to attempt crawling in and out of a small tent.

The Rockley Park minibus was parked at the stage end of the marquee, and Tara's father was there, talking to Mr. Lowther.

"Hi there, sweetie!" he said as soon as he caught sight of Tara. "I brought your bass, and your tent. They're in the bus."

"Thanks," said Tara. "Does anyone mind if I put the tent up now?"

"There are loads of us here to help with the equipment," Danny said. "So you go ahead."

Tara hauled her tent out of the bus, and then she and Pop disappeared off to the camp to put it up. Meanwhile, Judge Jim unlocked the double doors at the back of the bus so they could unload. There was a small entrance at the back of the stage so they wouldn't get in the way of the marquee people, who were still working in the main part of it.

There was a mass of heavy cables to unload, as well as the mixing desk and several amps, not to mention a whole heap of microphones.

"Shall I set up the drums?" asked Danny, spying a set of drum microphones. "They're at the side of the stage."

"Good idea," agreed Judge Jim. "Then you can fix up the drum mics, ready for us to test the system."

Soon, everyone was busy and, by the time Tara and Pop came back from erecting Tara's tent, the stage was full of equipment. Cables were snaking everywhere, with Fitz and Judge Jim busy making connections. The boys were lugging equipment into place, Danny had almost finished putting up the smart, silvery drum kit, and Chloe and Lolly were wrestling with several bits of chrome tubing.

"I can't get this wing nut undone," Chloe complained.

Marmalade had a try. "There you are," he told her, handing it back, well loosened. "All you needed was a man with strong muscles." He flexed his arm muscles and Chloe gave him a playful punch.

"Thanks," she said, slotting one piece of tubing into another. She adjusted the length and opened the feet at the other end of the tube. "Ta-da!" she announced. "One microphone stand. Where shall I put it?"

Judge Jim looked up from the cables he was sorting out. "That's probably the best one we've got for vocalists," he told her.

"I'll put it centre stage at the front then," she said.

A while later Mr. Lowther came out with some

drinks. He handed one each to Judge Jim and Fitz and they sat on the edge of the stage chatting, while the students fetched themselves soft drinks from the kitchen.

"We'll be able to get powered up this afternoon," said Ed happily.

"I can't wait to start playing again," said Ben. "I know it hasn't been long, but I've really missed the band."

Everyone felt the same, so after a quick lunch they all gathered in the marquee. Tara had slung the black strap of her beloved Rickenbacker over her shoulder and Ed quickly retuned one of the strings on his guitar. Danny slid behind the drum kit and picked up his sticks, while Ben adjusted his effects pedal.

"Come on up," Ben told Chloe. "We'll need to test your microphone as well."

Jess and Marmalade watched as Chloe made her way up onto the little stage. "I've never seen Chloe perform live before," she said. "Not with Wizard Monkey Breath."

Marmalade smiled at her. "You're in for a treat then," he said. "I expect they'll only play a few bars at first, to get the sound levels right, but even though I've heard them loads of times, it's still exciting."

Tara's dad turned on the power, and Judge Jim stood at the mixing desk. To everyone's great disappointment, the lights on the mixing desk refused to come on. "We've got a loose connection somewhere," said Judge Jim.

The amps all worked, and most of the microphones were all right, but the mixing desk was essential, and it was proving tricky to get going. A couple of times it started working but then the connection failed again.

"There's nothing for it," Judge Jim sighed. 'We'll just have to check all the connections again."

"These things happen," said Chloe to Jess when she joined her offstage, but inwardly she was worried. What if Judge Jim *couldn't* get the mixing desk to work? It was an old one he'd had for ages. What if there was something wrong with the desk itself?

It would be a total disaster if they couldn't mix the sound properly.

Tara, Ed, Ben and Danny couldn't resist starting to jam. They'd been waiting around for too long. The amps were working fine, and the sound blared out of the practice speakers, but for once the usually calm Judge Jim lost his cool.

"I can't think straight with you lot playin'," he told them. "Go and do somethin' else while we fix this. If we can't get the desk workin' you won't be needing to practise because there won't be no performances!"

There was a shocked silence, and then the students melted quietly away, leaving Judge Jim and Tara's father in peace.

"I hope they *can* sort it," fretted Lolly as they all made their way to their camp. "Mum will be so annoyed if we can't perform. Since she's got used to the idea, she's been ringing everyone to tell them about it."

"Sebastian Walters will get it in the neck for suggesting the idea if it doesn't work," said Pop.

"I hope he doesn't spill the beans about it being me who put him up to it."

"And it'll be so embarrassing, us camping here for nothing," said Danny. "After all, the performance is the only reason we're here."

Every now and then one of them would go to the marquee to see how the men were getting on, but the news was never good.

"It's total silence in there," said Ben, having been to check halfway through the afternoon. "Apparently they think they've found the problem now, but they need more tape and some other stuff. They've gone into town to try and get it."

Jess looked at her watch. "Well the shops won't be open for much longer," she said. "What happens if they don't get the things they need?"

No one replied. Chloe looked at the camp. They had worked so hard at bringing the Rockley Park gang together, and they had such high expectations of the summer party. But if they couldn't perform they wouldn't be needed. They would just be in the way of a load of adults. Chloe didn't want to voice her thoughts, but she was sure everyone else was thinking the same thing. If they couldn't perform, the camp was over, and they'd all be going home.

At teatime, Fitz finally appeared at the camp.

"Well, it's not particularly good news," he told the waiting group. "There's only one little electrical shop in the nearest town, and they didn't have what we wanted. But we phoned a shop a few miles further away and they did. It was just too late to fetch it today."

"But it'll be okay tomorrow then?" asked Tara.

"We hope so," said her father. "But we won't actually know until we can try it. There might be more problems with the equipment that we haven't found yet." He looked very tired and disheartened.

Chloe found herself wanting to blame Judge Jim. He'd always been the one person who was so totally reliable in her life at school, and now he was the very one who was letting them down.

"Couldn't he have checked all this before he said he could help?" muttered Ben, as he stabbed a stick morosely into the ashes of the fire pit.

"Not really," Danny pointed out. "He's borrowed several bits and pieces to do this, and today is the first time they've all been put together."

"But it's his old mixing desk that's bust!" said Marmalade. "Why did he bring it if it's no good?"

"It was probably fine the last time he used it," said Tara loyally. "But it *is* old. Maybe bumping it along the road gave it a loose connection somewhere." She glared at Marmalade. "You're a dancer," she told him. "You just don't understand about technical things."

Marmalade looked annoyed and Chloe sighed. Everyone was scratchy today. It was such a shame. But she felt guilty for blaming Judge Jim. Even under the best of circumstances, things could go wrong with sound systems, and he had only been trying to help.

The atmosphere at the camp that evening was very muted. Mr. Lowther was needed for all sorts of last-minute party arrangements, and Fitz elected to camp out instead. He did his best to keep everyone cheerful, but he couldn't stop them feeling that they were all simply in the way. Judge Jim appeared for half an hour, but he soon made his excuses, and went in for an early night.

"He feels bad about the equipment not working," explained Fitz. "He's such a perfectionist, and I think he's annoyed about letting himself be talked into helping out when he knew it would be a bit of a fiddle to get right."

"That's my fault," said Tara dolefully. "I talked him into it."

Fitz put his arm around her. "Nobody's to blame," he told her. "It was a cracking idea. It's just unfortunate the way things have turned out."

It had been a long day, and pretty soon everyone was talking about going to bed. Chloe and Jess said goodnight to the others, zipped up the flaps of their tent, and snuggled into their sleeping bags.

"I'm sorry about today," Chloe whispered to Jess.

"Me too," replied Jess. "I wish I hadn't thought of it now."

"You weren't to know there'd be so many problems," said Chloe. "None of us were. Let's just hope it'll all be sorted out in the morning." Chloe crossed her fingers in her sleeping bag. It would be a miracle if everything worked, even once they had got the bits they needed. She could see that as soon as one problem had been fixed another might rear its head. Today had been frustrating enough, but tomorrow might be a nightmare.

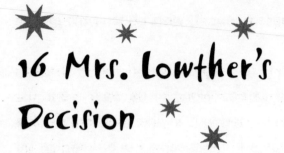

16 Mrs. Lowther's Decision

The next morning it was quite chilly when Chloe woke. She lay quietly for a few minutes, listening to a pigeon cooing in the tree just outside her tent. She was snug in her sleeping bag, but her nose was cold, and she didn't feel like getting up. But she needed the loo, so there was nothing for it – she had to. Reluctantly, she wriggled out of the warmth, and reached for a jumper to pull over her pyjamas. Her flip-flops were just outside the tent. They were spangled with dew and cold to her bare feet. She grimaced as she put them on. It was even chillier now she was outside. It was misty too. In fact, she could hardly see the house for the mist swirling about. The grass was soaked in dew, so she rolled her pyjama trousers up to avoid getting them wet.

By the time she got to the gardener's loo she was feeling decidedly cold. And when she looked into the mirror she could see drops of moisture glistening in her hair. They looked quite pretty, but she frowned at her reflection in the dim little mirror. What had happened to the hot summer weather?

On her way back to her tent she met Danny, looming out of the mist. "Where's the sun gone?" he asked. He was wearing shorts and flip-flops, and if Chloe had been in a better mood she'd have poked fun at him. But all she wanted to do was to crawl back inside her sleeping bag.

"Dunno," she muttered, hardly stopping.

Back in the tent Jess was just awake. She watched as Chloe slid her wet feet back into the sleeping bag and snuggled in, still wearing her thick jumper.

"What's it like out?" she asked sleepily.

"Horrible," said Chloe grumpily. "I'm going back to sleep."

But that was easier said than done. Although there was no sun it was still very light in the tent. And Chloe found herself listening to all the early morning sounds around her. More birds were singing now, and she could hear the occasional voice, as her friends started to get up and move about. Then she realized she was getting very overheated. She struggled to a sitting position and pulled off her jumper.

"Sorry," she mumbled, after bumping her arm into Jess's.

"'S'okay," said Jess, who was getting dressed. "We ought to take it in turns to dress really."

"I'm *not* getting dressed," Chloe told her grumpily, lying down again and pulling her sleeping bag up to her chin.

"Why not?" asked Jess, looking worried. "Aren't you well?"

"I'm just not getting up *now*," Chloe explained. She turned her back on her friend and closed her eyes.

"Oh. See you later then."

Chloe grunted. She listened as Jess unzipped the

tent and fastened the flap behind her. Then she could hear Jess's flip-flops swishing through the wet grass. She wished she wasn't so grumpy, but she had a bad feeling about today. The sound system probably wasn't going to work, they wouldn't be wanted, and they would all just be in the way.

But slowly, the morning noises made her want to be involved. The clatter of cutlery reminded her that she hadn't had breakfast, and when she heard Jess explaining to Lolly that Chloe was tired and wouldn't be appearing for a while, she wanted to contradict her. But she'd feel silly yelling through the tent to people she couldn't see. There was nothing for it. She'd have to get up.

By the time she was dressed, a hazy sunshine was beginning to dissolve the mist. Everyone was standing up to eat because the seats were sopping wet, but no one seemed to be quite as dispirited as Chloe.

"Crispies or cornflakes?" offered Ben with a grin. "No bacon today. The fire's out, but there's loads of milk."

"Crispies, thanks," said Chloe, taking a bowl and spoon from the little camping table Mr. Lowther had found for them..

"Ed's been over to the house already," Ben told her. "He's going to go into town with Judge Jim while I stay to help Tara's dad."

"You think you'll get it sorted?" asked Chloe.

"No point in giving up yet," replied Ben. "We've got all day."

"I suppose so," said Chloe. "Yes," she added, telling herself to think positive. "You're right. We have got all day."

Chloe's spirits lifted more and more as the sun grew stronger. Soon there were only a few wisps of mist left, and then the sun really broke through and the camp was flooded with warmth.

"That's better!" said Lolly, stretching in the golden light. "Are you okay, Chloe?"

"I'm okay now," she answered, not wanting to admit to her earlier misery. "I was just missing the sun."

"You and everyone else too!" laughed Lolly. "But

don't worry. The sun *always* shines on Mum's party day. I tell you, it doesn't dare do anything else! Shall we have some singing practice in a bit? We could do some voice exercises to warm our vocal cords up."

"Good idea," said Chloe, feeling much more enthusiastic about the day.

They were in the middle of clearing up after breakfast, when Chloe noticed an unexpected figure approaching. "It's Mrs. Lowther," she said.

Pop and Lolly looked up in surprise and Pop grimaced. "Oh dear," she said. "This doesn't look good. Mum ought to be far too busy to bother with us just now."

"Whatever can she want?" wondered Lolly.

Mrs. Lowther was wearing designer jeans and a gorgeous, cashmere jumper, which was beginning to look a little too hot in the warm sunshine. She was also sporting multicoloured wellies, which would normally have made Chloe want to snort with laughter. But something in the expression on Mrs. Lowther's face made Chloe realize this was deadly serious.

"Gather round, please," said Mrs. Lowther, flapping her hands awkwardly at them. "I just wanted to thank you all for coming at such short notice," she began. "It was good of you, and I do appreciate it. However, you must realize that events such as these take a lot of organizing, and nothing can be allowed to interrupt that organization."

Chloe felt as if a hole was growing in the pit of her stomach, and all her bad feelings about the day started coming back.

"I understand that there are problems with the sound system," Mrs. Lowther continued.

Danny and Chloe exchanged glances and Tara looked at her feet.

"I've told Mr. Jim Henson and your father, Tara, that they have until eleven-thirty this morning to resolve it," she said. "If it's not fixed by then I shall go back to my original plan of relying on the disco for entertainment. That will give you all plenty of time to clear your equipment out of the marquee."

"But Mum!" protested Pop.

"It'll only take a few minutes to clear things away, with all of us to help," said Lolly.

Mrs. Lowther waved her daughters' objections away. "Obviously, I can't expect you to leave this afternoon, and so the caterers will still supply your dinner in containers, which you can enjoy at your..." she waved her hands again, "camp." Mrs. Lowther looked rather embarrassed. "I would simply ask that you do not invade the marquee when the disco begins," she told them awkwardly. "My daughters will be able to explain that this party has never been designed for children. You will be able to hear the music from here, and can have your own party, quite separate from the adults." She smiled at them all, anxiously. "Which I expect you'd prefer anyway. Thank you again. And I hope you have a lovely time."

"Of course," muttered Chloe politely.

"That's fine," added Tara.

"Thanks," said Danny.

Mrs. Lowther smiled at them gratefully. "Thank you for your understanding," she told them. "Poppy and

Polly, can you come with me, please?"

Pop and Lolly followed their mother, looking very embarrassed.

"Well that's it then," said Tara crossly once they were out of earshot. "There's no way they can arrive back from town with the bits and get the sound system up and working in two hours flat."

She turned on her heel and headed for the marquee.

"Where's she going?" asked Jess.

"Maybe she's going to pack up a few mic stands," said Danny. "She'll feel really silly if they *do* get the sound working though. She'll just have to put them up again."

"But it's not all that likely, to be honest, is it?" said Chloe dolefully.

Danny bit his lip. "Two hours is no time at all," he agreed, "but we can't give up yet."

"You're right," agreed Jess. "You mustn't give up hope until there's no hope left."

Chloe shot a grateful look at her friend. Jess made

her feel guilty. Of course Jess and Danny were right, and she and Tara were wrong. There was still a chance – a slim one – but it was still there.

After about half an hour Lolly and Pop returned, carrying a long wooden box between them. They dumped it on the grass.

"Croquet set," explained Pop, looking thoroughly fed up. "Mum wants to keep you all busy so you don't, as she put it, 'get in the way'."

"We've got to go and put the guests' names on the place settings for her now," said Lolly apologetically. "She says she doesn't have time, and she doesn't trust anyone else to get it right."

Danny opened the long, wooden box and peered inside.

"But we don't know how to play croquet," said Marmalade, going over to join his friend.

"There are rules here, in the lid," Danny said, lifting out a couple of metal hoops. "And instructions on how to set it up."

Chloe and Jess looked at each other. Chloe didn't

particularly want to play croquet, and Jess didn't look too keen either.

"I tell you what," said Pop, noticing their expressions. "Why don't you come with us while we do the place names?"

"Good idea!" agreed Lolly. "I would feel terrible just abandoning you all morning."

"Well, if you're sure," said Chloe gratefully. "We really don't want to get in the way."

"Come on then," said Pop. "What about you, Jess?"

Jess looked undecided. "It's okay," she said after a moment. "I'll stay with the boys."

Marmalade shot her a grin and rolled a croquet ball towards her.

In Mr. Lowther's study, Lolly collected a basket full of beautifully printed name cards. Pop picked up a list that her mother had made, and studied it. "At a party of over two hundred people not everyone is best friends," she explained to Chloe. "So Mum always tries to make sure that enemies don't sit at the same table."

Lolly found herself laughing. "In case of fights!" she said.

Over in the marquee it was looking very festive. All the tables were up, with pink tablecloths laid and little gilt chairs placed around them. There were balloons, streamers and flowers everywhere, and a small dance floor had been laid in front of the stage, ready for the disco. Mrs. Lowther had already numbered the tables, so all the girls had to do was put the names in the correct places according to the list.

"Look! Sebastian Walters and his wife are next to Mum and Dad," said Lolly as they made a start.

"Poor them," said Pop darkly, going over to the stage.

Chloe followed. Judge Jim, Fitz and Ed were back and Ben and Tara were hard at work with them. But the stage was in chaos, and it seemed to Chloe as if the mixing desk was in pieces. Things didn't look good for the glittering entertainment that they had all hoped to provide.

"You got back quickly from the shop," said Pop. "Did you find the bits you needed?"

Ed looked up for a moment. "Yes," he said. Before he could add anything Judge Jim called for more gaffer tape, and Ed took him a roll.

"Better leave them to it," said Chloe.

"You're right," said Pop.

It took the girls quite a long time to set out all the names. When they'd finished, Tara joined them.

"I'm not doing any good here," she told them in a low voice. "I'd better come back with you." They took the basket back to the house, and went over to the camp. Marmalade and Jess were playing croquet, with Danny reading out the rules.

"It'll be lunchtime soon," Jess observed.

"What time *is* it?" asked Lolly.

Chloe pulled out her phone and looked. "Almost twelve," she said.

"That's it then," said Pop, aiming a kick at a croquet ball that had rolled close by. "No performance."

"Oi!" yelled Marmalade. "You've ruined my shot!"

"*Everything's* ruined," replied Pop, flopping down onto the grass. "It's past Mum's deadline."

Jess and the boys abandoned their game and joined the girls. Everyone looked serious.

"What now?" asked Marmalade. For once even he didn't seem able to make light of the situation.

"Well," said Pop disconsolately, "we'll be able to listen to the disco while we eat our supper."

"Oh dear!" said Lolly.

Everyone was fed up, but Chloe was frowning for another reason. "What's that?" she asked, looking puzzled. "I'm sure I heard something. Listen."

17 Fitz Plays the Blues

Tara looked up. "It's Dad," she said after a moment. "He's playing my song. They've obviously decided to give up, as the deadline has passed." She looked a bit embarrassed. "He's probably playing it for Judge Jim."

As the melancholy sound of the saxophone drifted through the warm air, Chloe found she was near to tears. Angrily she tried to shake off her feelings. Music had a habit of doing that to her sometimes. But then she looked at the others. They were feeling it too. The tune had triggered it, and the thought of having no performance, after they'd worked so hard to make it happen, was just too sad for words.

After a few moments the saxophone stopped. Then the strains of a bass guitar came drifting towards them.

"That's my Rickenbacker!" said Tara, sounding rather cross. She got to her feet and began to stomp off in the direction of the marquee, but before she'd gone far the sound stopped. Then the saxophone and bass started up together.

"Both instruments sound very rich," remarked Marmalade, his head on one side.

"Very balanced," agreed Danny with a quizzical expression on his face. "The saxophone and bass aren't drowning each other out at all."

Chloe stared at Tara. "You don't think...?"

But Tara had already set off at a run. "They've done it!" she yelled over her shoulder. "They've got the mixing desk working. I swear it's true!"

Everyone raced after Tara in a mad gallop to see who could get to the marquee first. Chloe found she was laughing as she ran, which slowed her down a bit. Marmalade, as the fittest of them all, sprinted past Tara and disappeared round the corner, closely followed by Jess.

By the time Chloe arrived, Marmalade was leading Jess in a slow, bluesy jazz dance in front of the stage. Her face was as pink as her hair, though somehow at the same time she seemed tremendously pleased. Onstage, Judge Jim and Tara's father were still playing Tara's song. When they got to the end of the verse, Judge Jim stopped playing and beckoned Tara over.

"We need a voice to mix in," he told her. "Come up and sing the lyrics, will you? Just to give us somethin' to work with."

"Okay." Tara climbed up onto the stage and approached the microphone stand that Chloe had put up the day before. She looked at Ben, who was manning the mixing desk, for instructions.

"Hang on a mo," he told her, twiddling a few knobs. "Okay. Go ahead, Tara."

Tara was a bassist by choice, and didn't sing solo very often, but she launched bravely into the first verse of her song. She'd performed the first couple of lines when Ben signalled to her. She stopped gratefully and waited.

"Okay," said Ben again. "Go for it!"

Fitz counted them in and all three began the song again. Chloe would have preferred a little less sax, and more voice, but Ben had chosen the levels, and no one could deny that the mixing desk was working very well.

"They've done it!" said Lolly, gleefully, giving Chloe a huge hug. "Thank goodness!"

"Come on," said Jess, disentangling herself from Marmalade's arms. "You all want to rehearse I know, so let's get going."

"Yes, Miss!" teased Marmalade. "Who's first?"

Jess blushed, but looked determined. She obviously hadn't forgotten that she'd been put in charge of organizing things. "I've got the running order here," she said, dragging a scruffy piece of paper out of her jeans' pocket. I was beginning to think I wouldn't need it."

Judge Jim and Fitz stopped playing and put down their instruments.

"I'll go and give the Lowthers the good news," said Fitz. "Well done, Jim!"

"Thanks for your help," Judge Jim replied. "We couldn' have done it without you." He clambered stiffly down from the stage and went over to the mixing desk.

"It just suddenly started working," Ben told him excitedly. "As soon as you began playing. All that rewiring must have done the trick."

"Well, let's hope we don't get any more loose connections," said Judge Jim with feeling. "There's not much time to practise onstage," he added to everyone. "We'll be needin' most of the time before the party starts for sound checkin'."

"Pop and Lolly are first up," said Jess, consulting her list. "Is that okay, you two?"

Pop nodded, thoroughly businesslike, now they needed to be professional. "Here's our backing CD, Ben," she said, picking it up off the table where the mixing desk was. "I put it there yesterday. I can hardly believe we're actually going to need it!"

"Ed and Ben are next," Jess announced, "with their first acoustic number. That right?"

"Yeah," said Ben. "No drums or vocals."

"I'll take over the mixin' desk," said Judge Jim. "I take it you'll be sittin' down to play your acoustics?"

Ed nodded. "Once Pop and Lolly have finished their song I'll adjust their mics for us."

Everyone was so excited, and suddenly full of energy. After such a dismal start to the day everything was coming right. Chloe caught Jess's eye and they grinned at each other.

"This is going to be the best night *ever,*" Jess told her with shining eyes. Then she suddenly looked shy. "Thanks so much for letting me come," she added.

"It was Pop and Lolly who invited you," Chloe reminded her. "I just passed the message on."

"But, you know…they wouldn't have asked me if you hadn't been coming," Jess insisted.

"Well it's just as well she was then," interrupted Pop breezily. "How would we have managed without our organizer? You got this whole thing off the ground!

Come on, Lolly," she added, before either Jess or Chloe could reply. "Hurry up!" Pop jumped up onto the stage and made for the microphone.

"You've got the most brilliant friends," said Jess.

"Yes I have," agreed Chloe, and gave Jess a hug. "Let's have a look at your list. Where did you put me?"

"Just before Marmalade's dance," Jess said. "I'm looking forward to watching him. And you're on again of course singing *Sky Blue* in the finale, with Wizard Monkey Breath."

Absolutely everyone was busy. If they weren't onstage they were thinking about their performance pieces, making sure they were word, note and step perfect. It wasn't until late in the afternoon that Chloe suddenly let out a squeal.

"We haven't made decisions about our outfits," she cried. "And the guests will be arriving soon!"

"It doesn't really matter what we wear," said Tara with a sniff. "We've been camping for goodness' sake!"

"Well it matters to us," said Lolly.

"Thank goodness the fire has gone out," said Pop,

with a grin. "Imagine if we turned up to Mum's party reeking of woodsmoke!"

Lolly looked horrified. "We've done our soundchecks," she said. "And Jess, you must have a few moments to spare now. Let's go and get sorted out."

"Good idea," said Pop. "Come on. Let's get going."

"After all," said Lolly, "Pop and I are going to have to look a bit glamorous, or Mum will kill us."

"And our agent, Satin Fountain-Blowers, will be here," added Pop. "She'll be appalled if we don't make some sort of effort. Besides. It's fun dressing up, even when you're a model!"

"I know you don't dress up, Tara," said Chloe. "But won't you come with us? At least you could give us an opinion on what we try on."

"Okay," said Tara. "I don't mind doing that. And actually I will need to shower and change. Even I can't carry on wearing these grungy shorts."

"We can soon find something for you," said Lolly helpfully. "It's lucky we're all a similar size."

"Yes," agreed Chloe. "After all, when we packed we didn't think we'd be performing at a party, did we?"

"A lot has happened since then," said Jess.

The girls looked around them. The marquee was glowing in the late afternoon sun. The tables glittered with crystal glasses and silver cutlery. There were flowers everywhere, and delicious smells were beginning to waft out of the catering tent. Onstage, the silvery drum kit took pride of place, while several guitars waited on their stands, including Tara's beloved Rickenbacker bass. The microphones were ready. All they needed was the audience.

The boys had brought suitable clothes with them, and Mr. Lowther had suggested they shower and get changed in his dressing room. The friends went into the house together, so that Pop and Lolly could show the boys the way.

"See you later then," said Danny, as Chloe and the rest of the girls turned to go along to the twins' room.

"Oh! I haven't told you," Lolly called to the boys,

"Mum said could we all meet downstairs in the hall when we're ready. She's got a surprise for you all."

"What is it?" asked Marmalade.

"It wouldn't be a surprise if we told you," said Pop with a laugh. She took Jess's arm and grinned at Tara. "Come on, you lot," she urged the girls. "We need to get a move on!"

18 Party Time

Up in Pop and Lolly's rooms it was quiet and peaceful. Pop threw open the doors to the walk-in wardrobe and looked thoughtfully at her sister. "Do you think it would be a good idea if we wore our saris?"

Lolly smiled. "I think that would make Mum's night," she said. "We can so rarely be bothered, and you know how she loves it when we do."

"Okay," said Pop. "Let's do it as an extra little thank you from us for letting us have our friends here."

"What would you like to wear?" Pop asked Tara. "We must have something you like."

"No need," said Tara. "I got Dad to bring my new top and trousers when he came. They're in my case."

"Well!" said Pop. "That's impressive. I hope your dad got it right. If we asked *our* dad to bring clothes for us he wouldn't have a clue!"

Lolly giggled, but Pop was tapping her shoe impatiently. "We don't have time to mess about," she reminded her sister. "We need to get a move on, or we'll be late, especially as we have to put all the pleats in our saris."

Jess and Chloe hurriedly sifted through the clothes. Chloe chose a long, bright green dress, which went well with her strappy shoes, and Jess found a swirling, multicoloured silk minidress. The twins took identical, bright red and gold saris from a shelf and after quick showers they all got changed.

"That should really please Mum," said Lolly, standing in front of the long mirror to check her appearance. Pop was kneeling in front of her, deftly folding lots of beautifully straight pleats into the front of Lolly's sari.

"Do you have to do that every time you put it on?" asked Chloe, feeling very impressed.

"Yes," said Lolly. "You see a sari is just a long length of fabric. The elegance is all in the way you fold it and put it on."

Pop stood up and looked at her handiwork. "I think you did mine better," she said. "What do you reckon?" They stood together, arm in arm looking at their reflection.

Lolly threw the end of her sari over her shoulder and adjusted it carefully.

"I think you look absolutely stunning!" said Jess. "I've never seen anyone put a sari on before. I had no idea how complicated it was. And the fabric is so beautiful."

Chloe looked at the four sari-clad girls, two in the mirror and the two real ones. Pop and Lolly were wearing jewelled slippers, and lots of gold necklaces and bangles. The jewellery picked up the gold threads in the silk and made it glitter. They looked like a pair of exotic butterflies.

"You two look perfect as well," Pop said to Chloe and Jess. Then she turned to have a look at Tara.

"You look amazing!"

The others turned round in surprise. Tara had showered, thrown on a pair of black, satin trousers and a top, and rubbed her cropped hair so it stood out at all angles. Apart from a little eye make-up and lipgloss, her pale face was unadorned. Even so, Tara *did* look amazing.

"Stop it," Tara protested, embarrassed. "I can't look amazing. I always wear black, don't I? What's so different?"

Pop looked at her properly. "You seem so grown up," she said, sounding surprised. "Usually, in your black jeans and T-shirt you just look like any other tomboy. But that outfit must have been expensive, and it shows in the cut, the way the trousers and top fit you so perfectly. You're really cool, and with so little effort too. Fantastic!"

"Oh." Tara looked as if she wasn't sure whether to be annoyed or not. Then a happy smile crossed her face. "Thanks!"

"We ought to get over to the camp for our supper," said Jess. "Or we'll miss the food…and it smells so delicious."

"No, you don't need to do that," said Lolly. "That's the surprise! Mum had a change of heart when she heard us running through our songs. She said you must all eat and be at the party with us. That's why she wants you in the hall for drinks in a few minutes' time. You aren't just entertainers any more. You're all guests too!"

Chloe put her hands to her mouth, and Jess looked equally stunned. "Really?"

Pop grinned. "Really. Mum's had a bit of a shuffle round with places. Unfortunately, Lolly and I have got to entertain our agent and a couple of other people. But she got the caterers to squeeze an extra table in for us, and so we'll join you as soon as we can get away."

"Wow!" said Chloe. "Now I'm even more excited than I was before! And it's just what you wanted, isn't it? To invite some of your friends."

"Yep!" said Lolly with a grin. "Guests at the party of the year. I hope that's all right."

"It better had be," said Pop. She had gone to the window and was looking out. There was the scrunch of gravel, and the sound of car doors being slammed. "It's too late to back out now. And why would you want to?" she added with an excited smile, looking back at the girls. "The first guests are here!"

Suddenly, Chloe was nervous. She would hardly know a soul. Would anyone want to speak to her? And if they did, what on earth would she say in reply? But then she glanced at Jess and was reassured. Jess knew even fewer people, and she didn't seem scared. In fact she was glowing with excitement. Besides, they would be on the same table. It would be fine.

They made their way downstairs together. Judge Jim and Tara's dad were there in the hall, both looking very smart in black ties and dark suits. Mr. and Mrs. Lowther were there too, talking to a small group of people who had just arrived. Leela Lowther looked up and caught sight of the girls. For a moment she simply stared at the twins with a pleased expression on her face. Then she clapped her hands and laughed. She looked thrilled to bits with her daughters.

"Wonderful!" she said. "I was just telling Sophie here

about my girls. Here they are, Sophie!"

A large woman in a stiff, black dress turned to appraise Pop and Lolly.

"Here we go," muttered Pop out of the corner of her mouth. Chloe and Jess giggled.

Pop and Lolly were immediately pulled into a series of conversations with Mrs. Lowther's guests, and although the twins were totally polite, Chloe could tell that they'd much rather be with their friends. But in a way, Chloe didn't blame Mrs. Lowther. Who *wouldn't* want to show off such glamorous, famous children?

Tara, Chloe and Jess were left hesitating at the bottom of the stairs, but not for long. Soon Danny, Ed, Ben and Marmalade arrived, looking very smart. After a few moments, David Lowther came over to join them.

"Leela is a bit tied up at the moment," he told them. "But she did want you to know you're all invited to have dinner with the rest of the guests in the marquee. We couldn't have you staying in the camp while wearing all your finery."

"That's wonderful!"

"Thank you."

Chloe added her thanks to the chorus from her friends. She glanced over to Mrs. Lowther. To Chloe's discomfort, Leela Lowther caught her eye. The twins' mother smiled graciously at Chloe, but all the same, Chloe had the distinct feeling that Mrs. Lowther was tempted to come over and remind them all to behave. Fortunately a few more guests arrived and she moved away.

"Eating in the marquee is going to be great," said Marmalade, his eyes sparkling with pleasure. "We'll really feel part of things."

"It's going to be a really special night," said Danny.

Fitz greeted them with glasses of orange juice. And Chloe noticed several people carrying trays of drinks.

"The servers will bring you more soft drinks when you need them," said Mr. Lowther. "All you have to do is ask."

The hall was filling up, and they were being urged to move along the corridor, towards a tented passageway, which led from the house straight into the marquee. It can't have been properly dark outside, but the marquee was brightly lit, with spotlights on the empty stage and lots of large lamps everywhere. Above each table bobbed a pink and silver helium balloon, tethered to a flower arrangement.

"That's a good way to identify the tables," said Jess admiringly. "You can see the numbers on the balloons really easily."

"Except when a draught makes them spin round," said a woman behind her with a laugh.

Chloe smiled at her, and then the smile froze on her face. She'd seen the woman before. For a second Chloe thought that she must know her. Then she realized, she had seen her loads of times before on TV and at the cinema. The woman was an actress! Luckily she didn't seem to notice Chloe's confusion.

"I'm looking for table eight," she told Chloe. "Can you see it anywhere?"

"I can," volunteered Ed brightly. "It's over there by Judge Jim."

The actress craned her neck to see. "Oh yes!" she agreed. "I see. I hope I'm sitting next to Judge Jim

Henson. He's a legend, I love his music. If I'm not I'm going to swap name cards. Maybe he'll sign mine for me...if I ask very nicely!"

She smiled again and pushed her way through the crush of party guests.

"Did you see who that was?" Marmalade asked Jess.

"Of course!" said Jess. "And to think she wants Judge Jim's autograph. And I *know* him! Ooh, I am having a good time."

"Me too," said Chloe. She watched as the woman reached her table, pounced on a name card and swapped it with another.

"So much for Mrs. Lowther's careful plan!" giggled Jess.

"What's that noise?" asked Chloe. The sudden roaring and clattering was getting louder and louder outside. Chloe and Jess frowned at each other. They couldn't imagine what it could be.

"I expect it's Sebastian Walters's helicopter," said a man beside them.

"He's coming by helicopter?" said Jess, her eyes wide with astonishment.

"He usually does," confirmed the man, "when there's space to land."

The clatter got unbearably loud, and then faded to a whine. Now they knew what it was, it *did* sound like a helicopter. Chloe wished she could run outside to see it, but they were all being asked to take their seats.

"Oh. Right," said Jess. She looked at Chloe and rolled her eyes. "We are *so* out of our league here," Jess whispered to Chloe. "Isn't it brilliant!"

Then, when almost everyone was seated, Sebastian Walters arrived with his wife.

They oozed showbiz, as they picked their way between the tables, moving slowly towards their hosts, who stood up to greet them. They both gave Leela, Pop and Lolly enormous kisses on their cheeks, and as Sebastian released Pop she looked round, caught Chloe's eye and winked. Soon the Lowthers and their guests were sitting down, pretty well out of view.

Chloe and her friends had the best of both worlds

with a table just for them. They could feel part of the glittering party atmosphere, but as there were no adults on their table they could enjoy themselves without having to be on their very best behaviour. The food was utterly delicious, and there were so many courses! Their server was really nice. She even found an extra pudding for Danny, because he said that profiteroles were his favourite. By the time they were nibbling chocolates at the end of the meal, Chloe was sure she would never be hungry again.

"I'm glad I'm not on first," she told Jess contentedly. "I don't think I could sing a note at the moment."

"Well you'll have a bit of time to recover while the disco is going," said Jess.

The disco music was soon blasting out, but to begin with not many people seemed to want to dance. Eventually a balding man took to the floor, with a very thin lady who was wearing a gold dress that glittered as she moved. That got lots of others going, and soon the little dance floor was crowded, but there was no sign of Pop or Lolly.

Summer Spectacular

As the first disco session came to an end the sound of conversation was almost as loud as the music had been. People were getting up and wandering over to different tables to greet old friends. Coffee cups and wine glasses were being re-filled. All the empty plates had been cleared away. It was time.

Jess cleared her throat. "Is everyone ready?" she asked, pushing back her chair and getting up. "We'd better get moving."

To get to the backstage area they had to make their way back into the house and out through another door. All the adults were enjoying themselves so much that no one seemed to notice them leave. But the friends were all buzzing with excitement as they quietly took their places behind a curtain, off to one side.

"I can't wait to get started," Chloe whispered to Danny.

Jess took her list of acts out of her bag and looked anxious. "It's time Pop and Lolly were here," she said. "They're on first. But where are they?"

19 A Famous Night

Chloe was just about to offer to go and find them, when Pop and Lolly arrived.

"Sorry!" said Lolly. "People kept talking to us and we couldn't get away. But Judge Jim is at the mixing desk now, and we're all ready to rock!"

"Who's going to introduce you?" asked Jess.

Pop stared at her. "Well, you, of course," she said.

"Me?" Jess looked thunderstruck. "I can't do it!"

"Of course you can," said Tara. "You're the obvious person. Or are you going to give a performance too?"

"No!" said Jess. "But…I thought Judge Jim or your dad would be announcing the acts."

"But Judge Jim is at the mixing desk, isn't he?" Lolly said.

"And I've just noticed Mum over there," said Tara excitedly. "She's made it back from Poland in time!" Tara craned her neck to see better. "She and Dad look really happy," she said. "It's the first time they've been out together for ages. We can't break that up."

"Of course not," said Lolly. She put her arm round Jess. "You've been so good at organizing us," she said. "You know exactly who's doing what and when. You can do it, Jess."

"Of course you can," said Pop.

Jess looked at Chloe and Chloe blushed. "It didn't occur to me to think about it," she admitted. "Sorry. But you are by far the best person for the job, Jess. And it means you'll be part of the performance with us."

Jess looked from one to the other and then took a deep breath. "All right," she said, suddenly terribly nervous. "I'll do it."

Pop and Tara clapped her on the back.

"Well done!" said Chloe. "I'm really proud of you, Jess."

"You'll be great," Lolly added encouragingly.

"Do I look okay?" Jess asked, smoothing down her hair anxiously.

"You look lovely," said Marmalade, and she blushed.

"Right then," she said, clutching her list of acts. "I'm ready."

"Go for it!" said Chloe.

"Show Sebastian Walters how it's done!" said Ben.

The students all waited as Jess went out onto the stage. Chloe crossed her fingers, hoping the guests would take notice of her, but she needn't have worried, because as soon as Jess appeared under the spotlight people began to clap.

"I hope she waits until they stop," Lolly whispered to Chloe. "Or they won't hear what she's saying."

But Jess didn't need any help. As soon as the applause started to die away she raised her hand to ask for silence. And when she had the guests' attention she began.

"The students at Rockley Park school, which is where Pop and Lolly Lowther go, are going to entertain you now." Her voice sounded a bit wobbly.

"Hurrah!" came a loud cheer. It was unmistakably Sebastian Walters's voice. "Who's on first?"

"I was just about to tell you that," said Jess indignantly into the microphone.

There was a roar of laughter and when Jess spoke again it sounded as if the laughter had given her confidence. She was completely in control.

"They are famous, beautiful and talented," she said. "And they are going to sing *Lollipop Lullaby*, the song that was specially written for them. So give it up for Pop 'n' Lolly!"

Pop and Lolly ran onstage to huge cheers from the audience, and Jess came off. As the opening strains of the *Lollipop Lullaby* backing track belted out of the speakers, Jess looked at Chloe anxiously.

"Was that okay?" she asked.

Tara laughed. "You're a natural," she told Jess. "Your timing after the laughter was perfect. Don't take any nonsense from Sebastian. If you can stand up to him like that, without actually being rude they'll all love you. Well done!"

"Thanks!" Jess went pink with pleasure and relief.

It seemed no time at all before Chloe had to go on to sing her solo. She looked out at the audience. It was much smaller than some she had performed in front of. Here, she was so close she could see the expressions on people's faces, and hear the clink of coffee cups as they were gently returned to their saucers. It wasn't competitive, like at school, or scary, like at a large stadium or in a TV studio. But the spotlights shining down reminded her that it was still a serious performance, and she must give it all she'd got.

Although bathed in the hot lights Chloe still felt as if she was singing for friends. She performed the song very simply, keeping her voice low and intimate, but it was from the heart, and her emotion shone through.

As soon as she'd finished she fumbled slightly when putting the microphone back on its stand. For half a second she was afraid that they hadn't liked her song, but then the applause came, and it was deafening. Sebastian Walters even stood up and clapped with his hands above his head, grinning at her. Chloe blushed with pleasure, gave a bow and left the stage.

Marmalade got a huge cheer for the comic robot dance he'd choreographed for the end of term concert at school. When he came offstage he was dripping with sweat. "I'm having the *best* time," he told Jess. "But it's getting incredibly hot in there."

With so many people packed into the marquee, the strong lights, and the heat of the summer night, it *was* getting pretty airless. Luckily, others must have felt the same, because a few of the servers started to roll up the side panels of the marquee. Almost immediately, a gentle draught drifted in, cooling everyone down.

Ed and Ben went on again and performed an acoustic version of *Stairway to Heaven.* "That's the perfect number to follow Marmalade's dance," said Chloe to Jess. "You've got the running order just right."

"Thanks!" said Jess, with a beaming smile.

Tara and Fitz performed Tara's new song, with Danny on drums. Their laid-back jazz earned them big cheers.

"Some people even got up to dance during your song," Chloe said when Tara came backstage again. "They loved it."

"They've been a great audience," said Tara, happily. "They've liked everything so far, and thank goodness the sound system has kept working for us."

"Don't say that!" begged Chloe. "Keep your fingers crossed that it holds out until the end."

But it *was* getting towards the end of the entertainment now, and Judge Jim's mixing desk was behaving perfectly. It was time for Wizard Monkey Breath to take the stage, so Danny, Ed, Ben, Tara and Chloe waited backstage for Jess to introduce them. She started in a conversational tone.

"I always thought that Wizard Monkey Breath Scares the Horses was a daft name for a band," she told the audience.

"Me too!" someone yelled out.

"Seems I'm in good company," she replied to loud laughter. "But then they won the International Battle of the Bands competition," she went on. "And so maybe it wasn't as daft as it seemed. Anyway, you must have heard of them," she went on. "And I'm proud to call them my friends. Singing *Sky Blue* to wind up our entertainment, please welcome onstage Chloe, Tara, Ed, Ben and Danny. It's Wizard Monkey Breath!"

As the band began to play, Chloe could tell that the audience wasn't in the mood to listen quietly. A couple of people began to sing along to the first verse, and when it came to the chorus more guests belted it out. Chloe knew the song was popular, but hadn't dreamed so many of the guests would be able to sing along. She shot a look at Danny on the drums and was rewarded with one of his broad grins. Now, more and more of the guests were getting up and swaying to the beat.

Chloe took her microphone off its stand and crossed the stage to Tara. "Shall we give them an extra chorus at the end?" she suggested.

Tara nodded. "Go for it!" she replied. "Let's jam it,

and really make it rock!" Tara told Ben and Ed. Chloe let the audience sing a line for her, while she quickly spoke to Danny.

Soon, the band had upped the tempo, and the song became a glorious jam session. Chloe abandoned any thoughts of singing the song as Tara had written it. The poignancy of the words wasn't important now the music was rocking. So Chloe simply repeated the words "sky blue" at intervals, and the crowd yelled them back to her. Now hardly anyone was left sitting down. The guests were singing, cheering, dancing, clapping and swaying wildly to the music. Chloe had never seen anything like it. The little stage was vibrating with so many dancers bopping away. This was too good for anyone to miss.

"Come out and join us!" Chloe yelled to the others backstage. Pop, Lolly, Marmalade and Jess ran out and joined their friends onstage, to even more cheers from the audience.

When they eventually managed to bring the song to a close, the applause was thunderous. The band and friends had to keep taking more bows, and eventually they left the stage to whoops and cheers.

Backstage they all exchanged hugs. Chloe's eyes were shining. Their live entertainment was over, but she was still far too excited to feel calm.

"That was *amazing*!" she squealed above the noise of the disco, which has restarted.

"They *loved* us!" laughed Pop.

"Did you see your mum and dad dancing?" said Jess.

"Yes!" said Lolly. "And Tara's too. I think our performance has probably convinced Mum that live entertainment is the way to go."

"I feel like dancing to the disco," said Marmalade. "But there's no room on the dance floor."

Jess peered out from behind the curtain. "People are spilling out onto the terrace to dance," she said. "There's plenty of space out there."

Marmalade looked out and laughed. "You're right," he said. "It was good thinking to roll up the marquee wall. There's loads of space outside, and it's not so hot either. Come on, Jess. Did I ever tell you what a cool disco dancer I am?" Without waiting for an answer he grabbed her hand and dragged her out to the terrace.

"Well!" Pop looked disgruntled. "*I* was going to ask Marmalade to dance," she said. She looked at the remaining boys. "Come on then, Ed," she laughed. "You'll do."

Soon all the friends were dancing in the warm night air. There wasn't really any need for partners. They danced in a big group, and kept going until the music turned slow and romantic for the very last song.

"Shall we go back to the camp now?" suggested Ben. "The adults will all start sitting down and talking again. We might as well do that in our own place."

"Good thinking," said Lolly. "I hate the tail end of parties, when all the decorations look crumpled and the tables are full of clutter. And I'm thirsty. Let's grab some drinks and take them back to the camp, where it's a bit more peaceful."

"Where are Jess and Marmalade?" asked Danny,

looking around. "We ought to tell them we're going back."

Ed pointed back at the terrace. Marmalade and Jess were dancing together, to the slow, final song.

"Ah!" said Lolly. "How nice. Don't tease them, anybody. It's lovely to have a romantic end to the evening."

"I thought they were getting on rather well," said Ben with a grin.

On the way back to the camp they passed Sebastian Walters's helicopter. It had landed on the wide lawn to the side of the house, where its pilot was looking after it.

"One day we'll probably be going to parties by helicopter," said Danny to Chloe.

"No way," said Chloe. "There isn't room for one in our tiny back garden. Besides, its rotors would blow all the sand out of my little brother's sandpit!"

Back at the camp, they were more than ready to sit down. To everyone's delight, Mr. Lowther had found some fairy lights, and had strung them in the nearby trees. It was lovely sitting on the bales under their own little twinkling lights, and looking back at the illuminated marquee.

"This has been a *wonderful* night," Jess told Chloe when she and Marmalade arrived a few minutes later.

"What would you have been doing if you hadn't come here?" asked Pop.

"Oh, going to the park, swimming, shopping, and staying with Chloe for a bit," said Jess. "We didn't have any evenings planned for when we were together, did we, Chloe? Except maybe going to a film."

"Well, you'll still be able to do that when you get home," said Lolly.

"But I don't want to think about going home yet," said Jess with a sigh.

Chloe wasn't quite ready to stop singing. Quietly, almost to herself, she began humming Tara's new song. She filled in the words when she could remember them, but after a few bars the others joined in, and with Tara's help the words soon came right. The bluesy feel was perfect. They were all happily mellow now. Ed slipped away to fetch an acoustic guitar, and Tara and Ben did the same. The sound floated up into the night sky and drifted away on the gentle night-time breeze.

All at once, from the direction of the marquee came some answering notes from Fitz's sax. It was a magical moment that sent a delicious tingle up Chloe's spine.

They sang on into the night, and the wail of the saxophone, along with the guitars, kept them company. At last, the notes from the saxophone died away. It was very late. Ed, Ben and Tara put their instruments down and Lolly fetched some rugs to keep out the late-night chill. Cocooned in the rugs they were all feeling sleepy. The lights turned off in the marquee, and one by one the house lights went out too. Only the colourful fairy lights were still on, casting a gentle radiance over the scene. Chloe and her friends fell silent as an owl hooted nearby and a fox barked in the distance. Then Lolly spoke.

"Don't lose touch with us will you, Jess," she said, "when you go home."

"I want to know when you get picked to play hockey for the nation," said Pop. "We'll come and support you."

"And there's the Olympics in a few years," Chloe reminded them. "Maybe she'll make that team too!"

Jess nudged Chloe crossly. "I've only just been picked to play for the *county*," she said.

"Ah, but aim high," said Tara. "Who knows where you might end up."

"She's right," said Pop. "Always aim high. If you don't try, there's no way you'll do anything."

"But what if I try and fail?" said Jess. "Wouldn't that be terrible?"

"No way!" said Tara. "Look at me. My ambition was to be the best rock bassist in the world. I'll never manage that. But it's through trying that I've discovered how much I love songwriting. You never know where ambition might lead you."

"She's right," said Danny. "It's always better to give life everything you've got. That way you'll find out what it is you really want."

"Okay then!" said Jess. "I'll aim high. Olympics here I come!"

"And if you don't make it as an international hockey player," said Marmalade, taking her hand and squeezing it, "I'll give you a job any time."

"Doing what exactly?" asked Pop.

"Oh I don't know," said Marmalade. "But I aim to be an incredibly successful dancer. I'll need *someone* to organize stuff and wash my practice clothes."

"MARMALADE!" Jess gave Marmalade a shove and he fell off his seat with a yelp.

"No WAY!" the girls yelled, and everyone laughed.

"Whatever the future brings," said Pop, when everyone had stopped laughing, "we must make sure we stay friends."

"And whatever we end up doing, we must support each other," added Lolly.

"A pact, a pact!" squealed Pop, startling everyone. "No, really," she insisted, calming down a bit. "We ought to make a pact to meet in ten years' time, and catch up with each other."

"Where shall we meet?" asked Ed. "Ten years is *ages*. We'll all be grown up by then. We could be anywhere in the world!"

"We can meet here," said Pop. "I bet Mum will still be having summer parties. I'll make sure you're all invited. If not..."

Lolly butted in. "We'll be grown-up," she said. "We can hold one ourselves, just for us."

"Write it down," urged Marmalade, taking his seat next to Jess again. "And we'll all sign it. Then we're more likely to stick to it."

Jess dragged the crumpled running order out of her bag and smoothed it out on her knee. Ben passed her a pen. She turned the paper over and looked up. "What shall I write?" she asked.

"We, the undersigned," began Pop.

"Agree to meet at the Lowthers' country home," said Lolly.

"Exactly ten years from now," said Chloe.

"To keep our friendship going?" suggested Jess.

Danny nodded.

"And to find out what we're all up to," finished Marmalade with a grin.

They passed the paper round and everybody signed their names at the bottom. Then Jess added the day, month and year. For a few moments everyone was lost in their own thoughts as the last embers of the fire glowed in the night. Then Marmalade cleared his throat.

"We ought to have a toast," he said.

"Good idea!" said Danny. "You always have toast with Marmalade."

While everyone groaned at the joke, he and Chloe filled everyone's glasses. Then they all waited.

"Go on, Marmalade," said Pop. "It was your idea."

Marmalade frowned. "How about...friends for ever?"

Everyone agreed and raised their glasses. Their voices rang out in the cool summer night: "FRIENDS FOR EVER!"

✳ So you want
to be a pop star?
✳

Turn the page to read some top tips
on how to make your dreams
✳ come true... ✳

✳ Making it in the music biz ✳

Think you've got tons of talent?
Well, music maestro Judge Jim Henson,
Head of Rock at top talent academy Rockley
Park, has put together his hot tips to help
you become a superstar…

✳ Number One Rule: Be positive!
You've got to believe in yourself.

✳ Be active! Join your school choir
or form your own band.

✳ Be different! Don't be afraid to stand
out from the crowd.

✳ Be determined! Work hard and stay focused.

✳ Be creative! Try writing your own material –
it will say something unique about you.

✳ Be patient! Don't give up if things
don't happen overnight.

✳ Be ready to seize opportunities
when they come along.

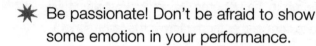 Be versatile! Don't have a one-track mind – try out new things and gain as many skills as you can.

 Be passionate! Don't be afraid to show some emotion in your performance.

Be sure to watch, listen and learn all the time. .

 Be willing to help others. You'll learn more that way.

Be smart! Don't neglect your schoolwork.

 Be cool and don't get big-headed! Everyone needs friends, so don't leave them behind.

Always stay true to yourself.

And finally, and most importantly, enjoy what you do!

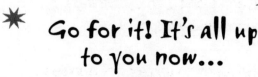

Go for it! It's all up to you now...

Usborne Quicklinks

For links to exciting websites where you can find out more about becoming a pop star and even practise your singing with online karaoke, go to the Usborne Quicklinks Website at www.usborne-quicklinks.com and enter the keywords fame school.

Internet safety

When using the Internet make sure you follow these safety guidelines:

 Ask an adult's permission before using the Internet.

 Never give out personal information, such as your name, address or telephone number.

 If a website asks you to type in your name or e-mail address, check with an adult first.

 If you receive an e-mail from someone you don't know, do not reply to it.

For more

read these other
fabulous books...

Reach for the Stars

Chloe loves singing and spends hours practising in her bedroom. So when she gets the chance to audition for Rockley Park – the school for wannabe pop stars – Chloe's determined to make the grade. But first she has to persuade her parents that her ambition is for real...

Will Chloe get to live her dream?

ISBN 9780746061176

Rising Star

Chloe's made it into top talent academy Rockley Park, and she's desperate to perform in the school's Rising Stars concert – she's heard that talent scouts often turn up from the big record companies. But she's got one problem...she can't find her voice!

Will Chloe miss her Big Chance?

ISBN 9780746061183

Secret Ambition

A TV crew is coming to Rockley Park school and model twins Pop 'n' Lolly are the star attraction. The talented twosome are used to doing everything together and they make the perfect double act. So Pop can't understand why Lolly seems so fed up.

Will Pop discover Lolly's secret before she ruins their glittering career?

ISBN 9780746061206

Rivals!

Talented drummer Danny is in constant demand at Rockley Park. But Charlie, the other drummer in his year, is jealous of Danny's success. Tension mounts between the two rivals, so when they're forced to play together in the school concert sparks could fly!

Who will come out on top?

ISBN 9780746061190

Tara is following her dream of becoming a rock star at Rockley Park. And when she hears about an African school for orphans, she decides that a charity CD would be a great way to raise money to help them.

Will Tara succeed or will she get herself into more trouble than she bargained for?

ISBN 9780746068359

Marmalade is one of the best dancers at Rockley Park. But he's also the class clown, and things get out of hand when a new boy arrives and Marmalade starts to show off even more than usual. It looks as though he's heading for a fall – literally!

Could this really be Marmalade's lucky break?

ISBN 9780746068366

Solo Star

Chloe's thrilled when she hears she's been chosen to appear in the Rising Stars concert – the show is going to be on TV and this could be her big break! The only trouble is she has to perform with a band, when she's always wanted to be a solo star.

Will Chloe be able to shine onstage?

ISBN 9780746073032

Christmas Stars

Rockley Park is buzzing with festive fun. Chloe and her friends are rehearsing for the Christmas concert and they've planned a secret surprise for their favourite teacher, Judge Jim. But then there's some shocking news, and it seems he won't make the concert after all.

Can everyone pull together to make Judge Jim's Christmas really sparkle?

ISBN 9780746077429

Pop Diva

Twins Pop 'n' Lolly are already top models and now they've won a recording contract too. But Pop dreams of being a TV presenter and throws herself into this new obsession instead of concentrating on her singing. So when the girls get to record their new single, Pop's just not good enough.

Can Pop save her sparkling singing career?

ISBN 9780746073049

Battle of the Bands

Chloe's band has won a prized place in an international Battle of the Bands competition. Every little detail has to be absolutely perfect for their performance, as it will be shown on TV around the world. So when Chloe's show-stopping dress is lost, it's a complete disaster!
Do they still stand a chance of winning the Battle of the Bands?

ISBN 9780746078839

Star Maker

Since taking part in the Battle of the Bands, Tara's become a star at Rockley Park – and across the country too! Her band is set to play on TV and at a massive charity gig. But Charlie is jealous of her success and he's making Tara's life unbearable. The trouble is, when the band's drummer falls ill, Charlie is asked to play instead.
Can Tara stop feeling angry with Charlie and get the band through their biggest concert ever?

ISBN 9780746097151

Dancing Star

Marmalade has been selected to dance in a new pop video and he loves the costume he has to wear. He's even inspired to invent an outrageous theme for this year's Rockley Park school prom. But it isn't glamorous and his friends are not impressed. They want an evening of glitter and sparkle – a chance to dress up and shine!
Will Marmalade be the prom king or a party pooper?

ISBN 9780746097168

Cindy Jefferies' varied career has included being a Venetian-mask maker and a video DJ. Cindy decided to write *Fame School* after experiencing the ups and downs of her children, who have all been involved in the music business. Her insight into the lives of wannabe pop stars and her own musical background means that Cindy knows how exciting and demanding the quest for fame and fortune can be.

Cindy lives between town and country – with deer and foxes one side of her garden, and shops and buskers a few minutes' walk away from the other. Her ideas come from both sounds and silence.

To find out more about Cindy Jefferies, visit her website: www.cindyjefferies.co.uk